Karen McCombie

Illustrations
by
G McLean

Best wishes
Gill McLean

Knights of the Wobbly Table

Save Our School

GADZOOKS!

Knights of the Wobbly Table
First published 2016 in Great Britain by

Monkey Island Publishing
Dairy Cottage
Hurgill Road
Richmond
North Yorkshire
DL10 4SZ

ISBN 978-0-9930636-2-6

A CIP catalogue record of this book is available from the British library

MONKEY ISLAND
PUBLISHING

Contents

The Story

1   In the Shed   5
2   Spies   8
3   Weird Names   13
4   Lady Mum   18
5   Dad to the Rescue!   22
6   Sword Fights   26
7   Trusty Steeds   31
8   Back to School   34
9   Marvellous Meetings   38
10 History ...but not as we know it!   44
11 The Dragon is Coming!   46
12 The Moat   50
13 Surprise!   54
14 Get a Grip!   59
15 Preparations   63
16 The Day of the Dragon   66
17 Enter the Dragon   71
18 Boiling Oil   75
19 Jousting   79
20 To the Rescue   83
21 The Banquet Begins   87
22 How to Slay the Dragon   91
23 A Fire-breathing Dragon   95
24 After the Fire   99
25 Time for a Change   102

Glossary of knightly words and phrases
    (Karen's guide to knight-speak)   108
Find out about the author and illustrator   110

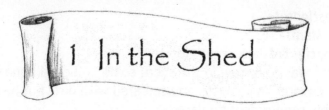

1 In the Shed

It was the almighty **CRASH** that sent Jack scuttling across the garden to hide behind the rabbit hutch.

He peered round the edge of the hutch, glad that no one had been there to witness his embarrassingly freakish terror! As he emerged, Benji (the rabbit) twitched her nose casually at him, as if to say:

'You total chicken!'

The crash had come from Dad's huge shed, down at the bottom of the garden. Dad never used it anymore. Not since he'd got his dream job, in London, with the theatre company. So, what on earth had caused the ear-splitting noise?

Maybe those old shelves had finally rotted and everything had tumbled to the ground. (Things like that did happen out of the blue.) But, as Jack moved closer, he could hear more clashing and crashing. Was an animal in there?

He crept closer, closer, closer. Curious, yet nervous.

He stopped.

Voices!

Voices?

How could anyone be in there? For the last few hours he'd been in the garden, kicking the ball into his goal. The garden was enclosed by a tall hedge with just a side path to the back. He would have seen anyone come round here.

What should he do?

Get Mum! The chicken on his right shoulder said.

Investigate! The explorer on his left shoulder told him.

Get Mum!

5

Investigate!

Get Mum!

Investigate! Jack crept closer.

There was a window in the shed, so he crouched beneath it. It was covered in cobwebs and smeared with dirt, but he could probably see inside if he dared.

He listened. Men's voices! He couldn't make out what they were saying though, because of the clashing and crashing. Were they burglars? What would they want in the shed? And *how* could they have got in there?

His fingers gripped the disgusting, cobwebby windowsill as he slowly pulled his face up to the glass.

He couldn't believe what he saw!

'Jack! Tea's ready!' Mum shouted, from the kitchen door.

No! Not now!

He hesitated. What if they got away while he was in the house?

'Jack! Tea!' Mum insisted. 'You've got football training in an hour. Hurry up!'

Argh! Football training! He loved football training but the men were bound to be gone by the time he got back. Why would they hang around in his shed for three hours? What were they doing there in the first place? Why? How? What? Who? A frenzy of questions bombarded his brain.

'JACK!'

'Coming Mum.'

He took one last peek inside the shed. He hadn't imagined it; they were still there. A startlingly good idea came to him. He darted across the lawn to the bike shed, pulled the lock off his bike, ran back and secured the shed door with it.

Aha! Now they couldn't escape!

Could they?

*

Tea was boring. Football was annoying. Sam Davis was being a show off and the coach shouted at Jack all through the match. He was itching to get home.

'Hey Connor!' he said to his best friend. 'Can you come back to mine? I've got something ... weird to show you.'

'Yeah okay,' Connor said, his mouth full of Mars bar, 'I'll just ask my dad.'

Connor only lived down the street from Jack, so his dad agreed.

'What's up?' Connor asked.

'Something in my dad's shed,' Jack said.

'What is it?'

'Some things that just ... appeared there this afternoon.'

Connor screwed up his face as if Jack had lost the plot. 'What?'

'Can't tell you. You won't believe me. I locked them in.'

'What? *Live* things?'

'Yeah.'

'Is it squirrels? Or rats? Or a snake!'

'Better than that. People.'

'People? In your shed and you locked them in? Are you crazy?' Connor said.

'Probably. But you have to help me.'

As they approached the shed, all was quiet and Jack suddenly wondered if he had just had a wild hallucination.

'Ready?' Jack whispered, as they crouched beneath the window.

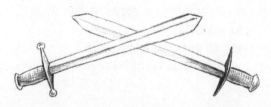

2 Spies

'Forsooth, Sir Trumpsalot, our situation is grave,' said a man, dressed as a knight, in not- so-shining armour. He was sitting on a pile of compost bags, with his helmet at his feet.

'Dost thou think I don't know this!' cried the other knight. 'Gadzooks, Sir Gaseehad, I am as distressed as thou art about it!' This knight was still wearing his helmet, with the visor up. He was pacing the small space.

'Pray tell; what is our plan of escape from this most filthy dungeon?' said the one called Sir Gaseehad.

'I know not. Perchance Sir Windibot may have an idea.'

The third knight was searching amongst Jack's dad's tools, and already had several strewn across the floor. 'Alas! I can find nothing with which to liberate us from this prison,' Sir Windibot said. 'I have tried everything I can think of, but it seems we are doomed to remain here for all time!'

'Be not so melodramatic, Sir,' said Sir Trumpsalot. 'We *will* find a way out of here. Let us try charging the door again.'

Jack and Connor ducked down under the window again.

'Unbelievable!' Connor said. 'How did they get there? And who are they?'

Jack shrugged.

'They talk funny,' said Connor.

Suddenly, there was a thunderous crash, making the shed shake, as the three knights ran against the door.

'Flippin' 'eck!' said Connor.

'They're trying to get out!' Jack said.

There was another crash as the knights charged again.

'We should let them out,' Connor said.

'Then what?' asked Jack.

'You can't keep them in there forever. It's kidnapping,' Connor said.

Jack frowned. 'We need a weapon before we open the door.'

They looked around the garden. Jack saw a rusty spade and Connor picked up a plant pot. They stood at the door to the shed. All had gone quiet.

'Go on. Open it,' Connor said, sticking the plant pot over his head (for protection of course).

Jack bent to flick the combination on the lock. As he did so, he heard a battle cry from inside.

'CHARGE!'

He jumped back just in time. But Connor, not being able to see, wobbled across the doorway as the knights tumbled out (in a heap of tarnished metal) right on top of him.

'God's breath!' exclaimed one of them. 'We did it!'

'Er, no,' came Connor's muffled voice from beneath the pile of knights, '*WE* did it! Now, *GET OFF ME* ... *please.*'

'I do believe we have crushed a knave,' said Sir Windibot.

The heap of tarnished metal clashed and crashed until Connor crawled out from underneath it.

'We are most heartily sorry, young knave,' said Sir Trumpsalot.

'Hi,' said Jack. 'I'm Jack and this is Connor.' He tried to sound breezy, but he still held up the spade, just in case.

'Kind sir, you have freed us, we are in thy debt!' said Sir Trumpsalot, bowing with a flourish.

'We are indeed,' Sir Gaseehad and Sir Windibot chorused.

The knights stood up. 'Pray, tell us the way to the castle and we will see that thou art handsomely rewarded.'

'The castle?' Jack asked.

'Indeed, young knave. Thou must know where it is.'

'Methinks he may not,' said Sir Gaseehad, looking around. 'We are in a foreign land, Sirs.'

'How did you get in Jack's shed?' asked Connor.

'Shed?' said Sir Windibot. 'That dungeon is called 'shed?' Strange. I have not come across such a place in all my crusades.'

'It's not a dungeon,' said Jack. 'It's where my dad keeps his tools and stuff he never uses.'

'Forsooth, we found some strange and mysterious contraptions in there,' said Sir Trumpsalot, glancing back at the lawnmower in particular. 'That creature looks fierce. I am glad it is sleeping.'

Connor and Jack exchanged confused glances.

'Are you hungry?' Jack asked.

'Truly, we are, young sir,' said Sir Windibot (the one with the biggest belly).

'I can get you some food, but you'd better stay in the shed for now. Don't want my mum seeing you. She might call the police.'

'The police? What are 'police'? Are they your enemies? Never fear! We will slay them!' Suddenly, all three knights drew out shining swords. Jack and Connor gasped, taking several steps back.

'Fear not, young sirs. You have saved us. We will not harm thee! On the contrary, we are sworn to protect thee,' declared Sir Trumpsalot.

'Oh ... right. Great!' said Connor.

'Just get back in the shed and we'll bring you some food,' Jack said.

'Of course,' Sir Gaseehad said. The three knights reversed, clankingly, into the shed.

Jack and Connor raced across the lawn into the kitchen. Fortunately, no one was about, so they helped themselves to food.

'Are they for real?' said Connor. 'They're so weird, like they're proper "King Arthur" knights.'

'I know,' Jack said, shoving some ham between two slices of bread. 'But it doesn't make sense.'

Connor was stuffing a load of chocolate biscuits into his pockets, when a voice from behind them said, 'Hungry are we?'

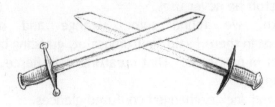

3 Weird Names

Jack's mum stood in the doorway, arms folded. Jack froze, two packets of crisps in each hand. Connor panicked and several biscuits dropped out of his pockets.

Jack tried a nervous grin. 'Er... yeah, Mum. Football makes you *really* hungry sometimes.'

'There's enough there to feed an army!'

The boys gave each other a knowing look.

'Okay Mum. We admit it. We're making a den in Dad's shed and a few 'friends' are in there already.'

'Hmmmm' Mum muttered. 'I thought I heard some strange noises earlier. Well just ask next time. Okay?'

'Yes Mum. Sorry.'

'Sorry Mrs. S.,' Connor added.

Jack's mum smiled, shook her head and went back to the sitting room.

The boys carried the huge picnic to the shed. They found the knights looking really fed up.

'We brought you a feast!' Jack declared, wanting to cheer them up.

'Thou art most kind,' Sir Trumpsalot said. The three knights, being chivalrous, offered everything to Connor and Jack first.

'No, it's all for you,' Jack protested.

'We might have a choccie biscuit though,' Connor said, helping himself.

'This is a delicious and most unusual banquet,' Sir Gaseehad said, holding up a bag of crisps and not knowing what to do with it.

'They're crisps,' Jack said. 'You open them like this.' He took

the bag and popped it, so it made a sudden bang.

'Saints alive!' yelled Sir Gaseehad, jumping back.

'Is it a weapon?' cried Sir Windibot.

Jack and Connor creased up with laughter. 'No, you eat them. Look inside. Taste them.'

Sir Gaseehad warily put his hand in the bag. He took out a crisp, examined it, then put it in his mouth. His eyes widened and his face screwed up.

Bleugh!
Pthwwwwh! Pthwwwwh!

Pieces of crisp sprayed across the shed.

'Salt and vinegar,' said Jack.

Sir Gaseehad put his fingers in his mouth and tried to wipe all traces of crisp from his tongue.

'So, who are you? And why do you talk so weirdly?' asked Connor.

'Forgive us for not introducing ourselves. My name is Sir Trumpsalot, this is Sir Gaseehad and this, Sir Windibot.' The three knights rose and bowed all at once 'And thou art ...Connor and Jack?'

'Yep,' Jack said. 'And the weird talking thing?'

'What dost thou mean by 'weird,' may I ask?' said Sir Windibot.

'Strange, odd ... you know,' Connor said.

'My dear fellow it is THOU who talks strangely, if I might be so bold. We speak as true knights should do.'

Connor and Jack shrugged. 'Don't meant to be rude, but you also have weird ... I mean strange names.'

'Alas! The Warlock, Wartfinger, has cursed us. We were on a quest for the king, (I don't even remember what it was now!) and Wartfinger (his arch enemy) played a cruel trick on us. He disguised himself as a beautiful maiden and invited us to take supper with him. As we hungrily devoured the banquet, our heads became fuzzy and our tummies began to make horrible gurgling noises. Suddenly the maiden turned back into Wartfinger, but we couldn't move. He cast a spell, changing our names to Trumpsalot, Gaseehad and Windibot, and making us forget our old ones. Our stomachs began to inflate, the gurgling got louder until quite suddenly, disgraceful, awful, RUDE, noisy jets of wind began to shoot from our bottoms!' As if to demonstrate, Sir Gaseehad gave a loud

PAAAARP!

And Sir Windibot, in answer to it, let out a whistling jet stream.

PHWEEEEEEEE!

Sir Trumpsalot squeezed his eyes tightly shut. 'As thou canst see, he gave us the sound effects to go with the names. All three of us are cursed to ...pass wind **very loudly** at the most inconvenient times!' The poor knight sat down, hanging his head. 'Oh the shame!'

Connor and Jack nearly burst with the effort of trying to control their giggles. They didn't dare look at each other.

Sir Gaseehad took up the story. 'Wartfinger thought this highly amusing. But to make sure we could not continue the king's quest, he banished us from the kingdom, sending us on the most terrifying journey. We tumbled through blackness and raging wind for what seemed an eternity. Then, we found ourselves here, in thy 'shed' dungeon.'

'But,' cried Sir Windibot, 'the worst of it is, our trusty horses were left behind and we may never see them again!'

'My poor Percy!' wailed Sir Trumpsalot. And to Jack and Connor's astonishment the knights burst into loud wailing tears.

Connor and Jack just stared at them, desperately trying to hold in their laughter.

Suddenly the sobbing and wailing was accompanied by another round of crazy bottom noises.

BLUFFFFWWWW!

PHWEEEEEE!

PTTTHHHHHT!

'Oh no!' wailed Sir Trumpsalot. 'The curse is upon us again!'

This was too much for Connor and Jack. They had to run out of the shed to collapse in a fit of giggles.

'This is awesome!' Connor laughed. 'Real live farting knights in your shed.'

'They're a bit wussy for knights though,' Jack said, trying to stop himself laughing. His stomach was aching. 'Listen to them crying!'

'And farting!' Connor added.

They collapsed into fits of giggles once more.

When the noises had died down, the boys went back into the shed, holding their noses. 'We can make you some beds for the night,' Jack said. 'Then in the morning we can try to help you.'

'That is very kind, young sir,' Sir Trumpsalot said, wiping his snotty nose on a gardening glove 'We are used to sleeping rough when on crusade.'

The knights and the boys pulled out some sacks and compost bags. The knights took off their heavy armour.

'Where dost thou live?' asked Sir Gaseehad.

'If you look out of the window, that's my house there. Connor lives down the street,' Jack said.

The knights peered out of the window. 'It is indeed a strange looking abode,' said Sir Windibot, 'Neither a castle nor a hovel.'

'It's just a house,' Jack said. 'We all live in houses.'

As the boys left, Connor said, 'Do you really think they time travelled here from medieval times?'

Jack shrugged.

'See you tomorrow,' Connor said. 'Glad it's half-term. We can hang out with the knights'

*

It was the middle of the night when Jack heard a creek on the stairs. He wouldn't normally wake, but the creek was followed by a CRASH, a loud PARP and an exclamation of 'God's breath!'

One of the knights!

His mum must have left the back door unlocked. (She often did!)

Leaping out of bed, Jack found Sir Windibot in a heap on the landing. Before he had time to speak, or shoo the knight back to the shed, his mum's bedroom door opened.

'What on earth ...' She stopped, seeing a man lying on the floor in metal trousers and a vest. 'A burglar! Jack! Get over here! I'll call the police!

4 Lady Mum

Don't move, buster!'

'No, wait Mum!' Jack said (wondering which American cop movie she'd got the word 'buster' from.) 'There's no need. He's a ... a friend of mine.'

'A friend? How can he be? Who is he?' She pulled Jack behind her and grabbed a heavy lamp from the bookcase. She braced herself, ready to smash it on the knight's head. He moved to stand up. 'Just you stay there, buster!' Mum said.

'Honestly Mum, he won't hurt us,' Jack said, trying to disarm his mother.

'Dear lady...' Sir Windibot began.

'Don't you 'dear lady' me!' Mum said.

The knight looked confused and tried again. 'Gracious lady? I merely seek the garderobe. My friends are content to use the shrubs but I am of a more delicate nature and decided that thy beautiful castle must have a garderobe.'

'What's a 'garderobe?' Is it like a ward-e-robe?' asked Jack.

'No,' said Mum, looking puzzled. 'It's a medieval word for a toilet. Jack, what is going on?'

By this time, Jack's sisters, Emily (aged five) and Cleo (thirteen) had come out onto the landing. Dad was away in London, as he often stayed overnight when rehearsing for a play.

'Mum!' Cleo exclaimed, seeing Sir Windibot.

'It's ok ... I think,' Mum said.

'Fear not, young damsel. I come in peace. In truth, I swear to protect thee, one and all, as thou art Jack's family.'

'Weirdo!' Cleo muttered, gathering Emily behind her.

'Let's go down to the kitchen and I can tell you the whole story,' said Jack, wondering how on earth he was going to convince them of the truth.

They sat around the wonky kitchen table, that Jack's dad still hadn't got round to fixing.

With the help of Sir Windibot, Jack tried to explain about the knights, but he could see that his family was not convinced.

'I will bring the others,' Sir Windibot volunteered.

He returned, followed by the other two knights, all wearing their not-so-shining armour (for effect, Jack thought).

Emily and Cleo stopped chattering and Mum stared, open mouthed.

'I see the womenfolk are impressed,' whispered Sir Gaseehad, smiling and bowing, with a flourish.

'Now do you believe me?' Jack said.

'I do!' Emily said.

Cleo looked suspiciously at the three knights, while Mum continued to stare.

'Dost thou have a garderobe, my Lady?' Sir Windibot asked, doing a little cross-legged, clanky dance, in his armour.

'It's down the corridor. Jack will show you.'

'My thanks,' Sir Windibot said.

'And just so you know, we call them toilets these days,' Mum added.

'My Ladies,' Sir Trumpsalot said, taking over the situation. 'I see we have shocked thee, but be assured, we are sworn to protect thee, as thy gallant son, Jack, rescued us from the shed-dungeon. Until we can find our way back to our own kingdom we will guard thy castle and thy very lives with our own.'

Sir Trumpsalot and Sir Gaseehad drew their swords in salute, making Emily screech and jump onto Mum's knee.

'Erm …We are very grateful Mr… Knight,' Mum said. 'But we really don't need …'

'Is this some sort of bizarre hostage situation?' Cleo hissed, behind her hand.

'I ...don't know,' Mum hissed back. 'Just play along.'

'Prithee, call us Sir Trumpsalot, Sir Gaseehad and the one in the garde..toilet is Sir Windibot.'

'Ok,' said Mum. 'But you'll have to go back to the shed now.'

'Thy hospitality is gracious,' Sir Trumpsalot said, as Sir Windibot returned.

'Weirdos!' Cleo muttered, as they left. 'You're not seriously going to let them stay in the shed? Call the police!'

'No!' Jack protested. 'They're not burglars or criminals.'

'I don't really know what to do.' Mum still looked dazed. 'I'll call dad in the morning. Let's get back to bed. I'll lock the door.'

'So, they can stay?' Jack asked, eagerly.

'Well ...' Mum said.

When Jack got back to his room he punched the air and said a quiet 'YES!' It could be fun having the knights around.

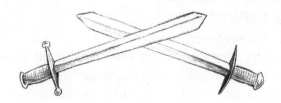

5 Dad to the Rescue

Early the next morning, Jack sneaked out to make sure the Knights hadn't just been some mad dream. He carried several slices of toast and a pot of tea out to the shed.

The knights were snoring loudly on their compost bags. Jack opened the shed door.

'Breakfast!' he shouted, as loudly as possible, then staggered back as the smell of three windy knights, shut in a shed for the night, hit him.

As if someone had flicked a switch, all three came alive at once. Sir Windibot fell off his sack with a clang and let out another enormous you-know-what.

'Oh! Oh! I do beg pardon!'

Sir Trumpsalot stretched.

PAAAAARRRP!

'ARGH! This wretched curse!'

'Don't worry,' Jack said. 'My friends do it all the time. And you should hear my dad! I've brought you some breakfast.'

'Thou art kind. Tis indeed time to break our fast,' Sir Trumpsalot said.

Sir Gaseehad bit into a slice of toast. 'This new age food is strange but delicious.'

'Will you teach me and Connor to sword fight?' Jack asked, looking at the three huge weapons propped up in the corner. The knights' armour may have been not-so-shiny but the swords were pristine.

'Why of course,' Sir Trumpsalot said. 'It would be an honour. You can be knights in training.'

'But only until we find the way back to our kingdom,' Sir Windibot said. 'Don't forget about that, Sir Trumpsalot. We must find Wartfinger and slay him.'

Connor poked his head around the door. 'You should pin him down and all three of you should sit on his head and do the biggest, loudest, longest trumps you've ever done, then ... slay the pants off him!'

Jack laughed and high-fived Connor. The knights looked at them strangely. Connor held up his hand to the knights. 'High five?'

'Is it a secret sign?' Sir Gaseehad asked.

'Not really,' Connor said. 'Just means we're mates, you know, friends. So, high five?'

Sir Gaseehad smiled and gave Connor a high five. The other two followed his example with lots of high-fiving and whooping.

'Now we are ... mates?' said Sir Gaseehad.

'Art thou not breaking thy fast, young knaves?' asked Sir Windibot.

'Okay,' said Jack, 'First of all, if we're going to be mates you have to call us Jack and Connor. Then try to talk like 21st century people. So instead of 'thou' say 'you' and instead of 'art' say 'are' and instead of 'thy' say 'your.' Get it?'

'I shall try. Are ... thou, I mean you ... not breaking thy, I mean, your fast?'

'That's it,' Jack said. 'And if you mean did we want breakfast, I already had some.'

'Me too,' Connor said.

'As you wish,' Sir Windibot said.

'I think you mean okay,' Connor said.

'O...kay,' Sir Windibot repeated slowly.

'See, we'll have you speaking 21st century in no time,' Jack said.

'Dost thou mean to tell me we are not in the 13th century anymore? That's impossible!' Sir Windibot exclaimed.

'Think about it. Nothing and no one looks or talks like the things and people you're used to,' said Connor.

'In faith, the boy is correct,' Sir Gaseehad exclaimed. 'And I rather like it.' He was tucking into his fifth piece of toast and slurping tea directly from the pot.

Sir Windibot looked horror-stricken.

'Be of good cheer, old fellow,' Sir Gaseehad said, slapping his friend on the back, 'Have a toast.' He shoved a slice into Sir Windibot's mouth, making him splutter and spew toast everywhere.

Sir Gaseehad chuckled, but Sir Trumpsalot gave him a stern look. 'Sir Gaseehad, this is not teaching the young knaves knightly conduct. Let us teach them some chivalry.'

'And sword fighting!' Jack said.

Out in the back garden, Sir Trumpsalot lined Connor and Jack up opposite Sir Gaseehad and Sir Windibot. 'Give them your swords,' he commanded. The knights stepped forward and ceremoniously handed the boys the swords. Both of them staggered and dropped the weapons.

'How do you swing those things? They weigh a ton!' Connor said.

'I see we will need practice swords for the present,' Sir Trumpsalot said. 'Do you have some?'

'That would be a no!' Jack said.

'Then we shall improvise,' Sir Trumpsalot said. He sent the other two knights back into the shed to find anything they could use as swords. They came back with a long handled trowel and fork.

'Not ideal, but they will do. Most knaves begin with wooden practice swords. Now, stand like this,' (he demonstrated) 'Sir Gaseehad and Sir Windibot: Advance!'

The knights raised their swords and stepped forward.

'Stop!' shouted a voice from the kitchen doorway. It was Jack's dad! 'Put down your weapons! Slowly now. Jack, Connor, back away.'

'But dad ...'

'It's okay Jack, I've got it covered,' Dad said, creeping exaggeratedly across the garden, his hand outstretched. (As if that could defend him from the sword-wielding knights.)

'My Lord Dad!' Sir Trumpsalot said. 'On my honour, do not fear.'

'Get away from my son! Back off! I'm warning you!'

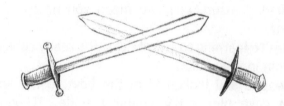

6 Sword Fights

'Dad!' Jack tried again.

Sir Gaseehad and Sir Windibot stood motionless, with their swords in the air, watching the strange little man advance.

'Lord Dad, I assure you, we mean you no harm,' said Sir Trumpsalot.

'Dad, we're learning to sword fight. It's really cool. Come on. You can join in if you like.'

Dad stopped and looked from the boys to the knights. Sir Gaseehad gave him a big beaming smile. 'Thou art most welcome, my Lord. I'm sure thou hast wielded many a sword.' Before Dad could say any more, Sir Gaseehad strode forward and placed the sword in dad's hands. Dad nearly dropped it but covered his embarrassment with a sort of Kung Fu twist, strange noises and a kicking sort of dance thing; finally dropping the sword with a flourish so it looked like a deliberate move. Luckily for him the sword stuck into the ground just in front of Sir Gaseehad. 'Zounds! Thou wilt have to teach me that move!' the knight exclaimed.

'Really?' Dad said.

'Verily, it is impressive!' Sir Gaseehad said, giving Dad a manly slap on the back that nearly sent him sprawling.

'As you wish,' Dad said, bowing with a flourish, his actor side coming out now.

After much clashing of swords with tools, Mum came to the back door, looking on in shock, to see Dad leaping around the garden, shouting 'En garde!' and 'Fie upon you!' and 'Come on, then!'

'David! What are you doing? I thought we were calling the police!'

'What? No!' Dad shouted, niftily twisting away from Sir Trumpsalot and clashing his long handled trowel with Sir Windibot's sword. 'This is so much fun!'

Jack and Connor had been cheering Dad on. Mum looked at Jack, shaking her head. He shrugged.

'Family meeting! Now!' Mum demanded.

Sheepishly, Dad put down his weapon. 'Sorry chaps, got to go. The Lady of the house requests my company.'

'Of course,' Sir Trumpsalot said. All three knights bowed with a flourish towards Mum. Her cheeks flushed pink and Jack was sure he saw a hint of a smile, despite the folded arms and the I-am-being-stern look. 'We will retire to our shed-abode and make plans to find the way back to our kingdom.'

'And I'll see you later,' said Connor, looking warily at Jack's mum.

*

'So, you dash home at the crack of dawn from London, when I tell you we had intruders in the night, and they're camped out in our shed, only to play sword fights in the garden with them!'

Dad, Jack and Mum sat around the kitchen table.

If looking sheepish could turn you into a sheep, then Dad would now be covered in a thick woolly coat and bleating 'Baa baa baa!'

'Mum, I told you they're not dangerous criminals. They've been catapulted here from medieval times,' Jack said.

Mum gave Jack her best sarcastic smile.

'Well what other explanation is there for the way they talk, the way they dress and how they got to be there all of a sudden, when I was in the back garden the whole time?'

Mum's turn to be speechless.

'Maybe it's true,' Dad said, his eyes lighting up as they always did when he liked an idea. 'They are expert swordsmen. And their lingo is spot-on medieval.' He began to behave all actory. 'Forsooth I tell thee, thou art the most beautiful and fair maiden in the whole of the kingdom!' Dad grabbed Mum's hand and kissed it several times.

Jack laughed.

'So what are we going to do then Sir Twitalot?' Mum said.

'How about we let them stay for a while 'til we find out how to help them get back home?' Jack suggested.

Mum was doubtful.

'Please Mum. Go on, *pleeeeeeese!* That would be so cool. Love you forever.'

'Well, they would have to stay in the shed. I'm not having them clanking around the house. And they would have to do some jobs to earn their keep, if we're going to feed them,' Mum said.

'Yay! It's sorted then,' Jack shouted, jumping up and kissing his Mum on the cheek. 'Come on Dad, let's do some more sword fighting!'

Mum gave Dad a look.

'I'll have to give it a miss, son. I've got to get back to London. I'm missing rehearsals as it is. Marcus will kill me if I don't get back. Tell the knights I'm looking forward to more training on my day off.'

Connor and Jack spent the rest of the half-term having fun with the knights. Cleo sometimes watched them from the kitchen and whenever the knights saw her they bowed respectfully; to which she would turn up her nose and flounce off, muttering 'weirdos!'

Emily, however, thought the knights were wonderful and they fell in love with her. Even Sir Windibot, who could be a bit of a whinge bag, could be seen on all fours, cantering around the garden, with Emily on his back, shouting 'Giddy up my trusty horsey!'

Mum made the shed cosier, with curtains, mattresses and garden chairs. She set up a portaloo behind it, which the knights called their gardeloo. She also gave them several gardening jobs to do, one of which was to mow the lawn. The lawnmower became known as Rotateeth. Sir Trumpsalot was very proud that he had tamed the monster, Rotateeth, and enjoyed 'taking him out for a walk' even when the grass couldn't get any shorter. His favourite thing to do was to make Rotateeth sneak up on Sir Windibot when he was having a sleep in a deck chair. Then he would make the monster roar suddenly. Poor Sir Windibot would jump up, trump loudly, and run away as fast as he could, being chased by a laughing Sir Trumpsalot and Rotateeth.

Sir Gaseehad spent most of his time following Mum around, doing any job she asked of him, flashing his charming smile at her and serenading her with ballads on Emily's ukulele. Mum was getting used to it.

Connor and Jack learnt to sword fight like pros, shout knightly phrases and shoot homemade arrows from a homemade bow into a practice dummy enemy. This was made from a sack stuffed with carrier bags, strung up to Mum's washing line pole. It had a turnip head, with eyes and mouth drawn on in felt tip, 'for realism,' according to Connor.

Sir Windibot was keen to teach them to skin the pet rabbit, but Jack didn't think Benji would be too keen on becoming dinner and a pair of gloves. Sir Gaseehad tried to teach them some love ballads to sing to their sweethearts, but Connor explained that 'girls stink,' which made Sir Trumpsalot ask if girls in the 21st century had the same curse as the knights.

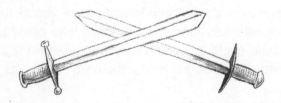

7 Trusty Steeds

Towards the end of half-term Jack came into the shed one morning. He took several gulps of fresh air and placed a clothes peg on his nose before entering. The noxious smell in the mornings seemed to be getting worse. He found the knights looking very glum.

'What's up?' he asked.

Sir Windibot looked at the ceiling.

Sir Trumpsalot tutted. 'Nay, Windibot, he doesn't mean, what's on the ceiling! He means; what is the problem? The problem is … we are missing our trusty steeds, Jack. We need horses, to feel like proper knights. How can we joust or run the gauntlet without them?'

'And how can we find our way back to our kingdom? 21st century to 13th century is a long way!' Sir Gaseehad said.

'I don't have any horses, but I have an idea,' said Jack. 'Wait here …' He ran out of the shed. Within ten minutes he was back. 'Come on you lot. I've got something to show you.' He led them round to the front of the garage. 'Meet your bikes.'

The knights looked on with puzzled expressions at the bikes. 'Are they alive?' Sir Windibot touched the red metal frame of the biggest bike, as if it might bite him.

'No. It's a sort of vehicle. Like a cart but with two wheels. And you pedal it,' Jack explained. The knights looked confused. 'Watch.' Jack got on a bike and began to whizz up and down the road. The knights watched in amazement.

'Such speed!' cried Sir Trumpsalot.

'Such elegance!' cried Sir Gaseehad.

'Such danger!' cried Sir Windibot.

The red bike was Dad's. It was the biggest. Sir Trumpsalot got on it. 'I shall call him Percy, after my own dear horse.' (He tried not to cry!)

The green bike was Mum's. It was a little smaller. Sir Gaseehad got on that. 'I shall call her Lady Susan, in honour of your Lady mother.'

The pink bike, with sparkly pedals and tassels on the handlebars, was Cleo's old bike. Sir Windibot (reluctantly) got on that. 'Do I have to?' he whinged.

'Yes!' everyone chorused.

'Give it a name Windi,' Sir Gaseehad said.

Sir Windibot pulled a face.

Sir Gaseehad guffawed with laughter. 'He shall call her Frillyfilly.'

'Enough!' commanded Sir Trumpsalot. 'Let us learn a new way of riding now.'

Sir Trumpsalot put both feet on the pedals at the same time and immediately keeled over to one side, crashing into the roses.

'Yowch!'

Sir Gaseehad sniggered. He gripped the handlebars, put one foot on a pedal and pushed off. Wobbling a little, he rode a few metres up the road. Then he twisted round in the saddle, 'This is how you ...'

SMACK!

He rode right into a lamp post and somersaulted over the handlebars, diving spectacularly into Mrs. Dobson's fish pond.

Jack and Connor howled with laughter. 'Your turn, Sir Windi.'

Sir Windibot sat in the saddle, his knees touching the handlebars, like a giant on an elf bike! He stuck out his bottom lip, gripped the handlebars, took a deep breath and pushed himself along with his feet on the pavement.

'That's cheating,' Jack said. 'Pedal.'

The knight put one foot on a pedal, closed his eyes and pushed off. Suddenly both feet were on the pedals and whizzing round, his knees nearly punching him in the face each time. But, Sir Windibot was off up the road at the speed of five antelopes (or maybe five tortoises).

'He's a natural!' Jack shouted, as the other two knights watched, rubbing their sore bits.

'Who'd have thought it?' Sir Trumpsalot said.

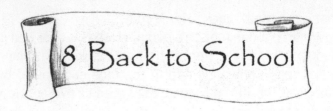

8 Back to School

Half-term was over. Jack and Connor were walking to school, feeling miserable. Normally they didn't mind school, but …

'Leaving the Knights sucks!' said Connor.

'Yeah!' Jack said. 'And they were upset this morning. I think it's really sinking in that we don't know how to get them back to their kingdom and that they might have to put up with the curse forever!'

'I wouldn't mind that curse,' Connor said. 'Imagine Miss Loopney's face if we could do big raspers like that, in assembly.'

This thought cheered them up and they practiced making trumping noises, using their armpits, all the way to school. Their school was called Dempsey Road Primary. In assembly, Miss Loopney, their head teacher, welcomed everyone back from half-term in her usual gushing way.

'I've missed you all so much my dears.' She took out a lace handkerchief and dabbed her eyes. 'Holidays are not much fun for me. The best part of my life is being with my *marvellous* pupils at Dempsey Road. But I hope you have had lots of fun. I'm sure you will share all your lovely experiences with your teachers. Now off you go and learn lots of *marvellous* things today!'

Jack was not sitting next to Connor, but he looked across at him, and both of them rolled their eyes. Everyone loved Miss Loopney, even though she was a bit zany.

Jack and Connor were in 5E. Mr. Eades, their teacher, announced that this half-term he had something special planned. He put on his dramatic, booming voice, whilst standing on top

of his desk and sticking his arm in the air like a superhero.

'This school needs a bit of a boost and our class is going to lead the way by being innovative and daring!'

The class frowned and groaned. Not another one of Mr. E's hair-brained schemes! Last year Mr. E's class had made an Amazon Rainforest along the corridor and in the classroom. Everyone got tangled in the creepers and eventually Mr. Stickler, the caretaker, in charge of health and safety, had forced him to take them all down. The year before, it had been 'Space – the final frontier,' with the windows blacked out, amazing solar system murals on the walls, and planets hanging from the ceiling. Mr. E. had insisted they do everything by torch light. Dangling planets hit the adults on the head every time they entered the room. But Miss Loopney had thought it was *marvellous!*

When they did 'a journey though the body', the whole corridor and classroom had been transformed into a huge maze of veins and organs. It got a bit gory when Mr. E. decided they should dissect a few real organs. Several mothers had protested and Mr. Stickler had stepped in again with his health and safety hat on.

Despite the frowning and groaning though, 5E couldn't help but be excited when Mr. E. had ideas.

'This half-term we are studying medieval times,' said Mr. Eades. 'So we are going to transform our classroom into a medieval castle!'

Jack and Connor's faces lit up.

In the shed, after school, Jack and Connor were explaining their idea to the knights. 'So we thought you could come into school and help us learn about medieval times. We could teach them sword fighting and all about castles and have jousting and feasting and battles and ... Mr. E. would be so up for it; he'd love it. And Miss Loopney would just say *marvellous!*'

'What kind of mystery are you talking about and up where?' asked Sir Windibot.

'Chill out, Windi,' (Sir Gaseehad was enjoying 21st century-speak). 'Myster-eeeeey is the strange name of their tutor. Maybe he is some sort of great wizard. And 'up for it' means he would like it. Right dudes?'

'Er ...yeah, Sir Gassy that's it,' Connor said.

'Well I think it would be splendid to help the young knaves learn more about our times,' Sir Trumpsalot said.

Jack spoke to his dad about the idea, on the phone that evening. Dad was very enthusiastic. 'It's a great idea Jack. It would really bring learning to life. I could tell your school that the knights are part of a travelling theatre company I know, and that they owe me a favour, so they'll come to the school for free.'

'So will you phone school tomorrow?'

'Even better, I'm home for a couple of days on Wednesday. I'll take the knights into school myself and introduce them to Miss Loopney. You ask Mr. Eades what he thinks, tomorrow.'

Mr. Eades was indeed 'up for it.'

'Sounds great, Jack. Just what this school needs.'

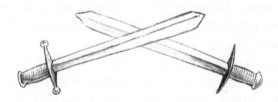

9 Marvellous Meetings

On Wednesday morning, Connor, Jack and his dad walked to school, followed by a very strange sight. Three men dressed in recently polished armour (including helmets) clanked up the street. With extreme difficulty, Jack had persuaded them that riding to school on their 'trusty steeds' would not be a good idea (especially the pink tasselled one)!

Miss Loopney was expecting them, as Dad had phoned her the day before. Jack and Connor had to go to class, but Dad and the knights sat in reception, being watched by the beady eyes of Mrs. Diamond, the school receptionist.

Miss Loopney waltzed out of her office at nine o'clock. 'Good morning, Mr. Sanders. And ... oh my! How *marvellous!* You've come in costume, gentlemen. Come in, come in! Mrs. Diamond, some coffee please. Or should we make that mead? Miss Loopney gave her famous laugh: A high pitched version of the Star Wars music.

'Ha-ha ha-haaaaa-ha!'

Long before the end of the meeting, Miss Loopney was won over by the charms and quirks of the three knights. The curse was kept mostly under control, although Sir Windibot had a few dodgy moments, and had to disguise the noise with loud coughing! Dad's proposal (typed up with aims, objectives and bullet points) was almost irrelevant. Mrs. Diamond could hear exclamations of 'Wonderful!' 'I love it!' 'Oh, my dear Sir Gaseehad!' and of course, at least fifty *Marvellouses!*

The knights were to start on Monday, working with all of year five on their medieval project. Their first task would be to teach the children about life in a medieval castle, and help them to transform their classroom into one. Dad took them along to meet Mr. E. and his class.

'They stay in role all the time,' Dad whispered to Mr. E. as the children gawped at the metallic men. Maisey Bates, renowned for her cry-babyness, burst into tears and Miss Cuticle, the teaching assistant had to hurry her out. The rest of the class gradually surrounded the knights in the middle of the room, and bombarded them with questions.

'They have strange names, but I'm sure it's just to make the kids laugh a lot. Oh, Laugh-a-lot!' Dad embarrassingly began chuckling at his unintentional, very dad-ish joke.

'Thanks a bunch for finding them for us, Mr. Sanders,' said Mr. E. 'What a bonus! We're really going to put Dempsey Road on the map this year, I can feel it.'

'Miss Loopney told me she'd like to get the local newspaper in,' Dad said.

'Great. We need some good press,' Mr. Eades sighed. 'It's been so negative recently, with the not-so-hot inspection reports. We're doing our best, but people are choosing Bottlington Avenue School over us these days.'

'Well this could be just what you need,' Dad said, patting Mr. E. on the shoulder in a cheer-up-old-chap way.

By now, everyone was talking at once, and the noise had reached unable-to-hear-a-thing levels. Mr. E. stood on his desk with his football hooter in his hand and honked it. That always shut everyone up at once. But it did give Maisey Bates another fright, and she had to be rushed from the room again.

'Right you lot, let the knights go. They'll be back on Monday to talk to us about life in a medieval castle, and generate lots of ideas for transforming this classroom!'

A cheer went up.

'Fare thee well,' 'Adieu,' 'Anon,' the knights chorused, as Dad ushered them out of the room.

'They are weird,' James said to Jack. 'But sooo cool! You are *sooo* lucky having them staying at your house.'

'Sir Trumpsalot is my favourite,' said Alex.

'I think Sir Windibot is really funny,' Ryan chipped in.

'Sir Gaseehad is our favourite,' said Jess and Katie.

'Did they really teach you to sword fight?' James asked.

'Yeah,' Connor said.

'Wow! Will they teach us?' Alex said.

'Course,' Jack replied.

'Come on now,' Mr. E. called. 'Everyone back to your seats. We're supposed to be doing literacy.'

Everyone groaned!

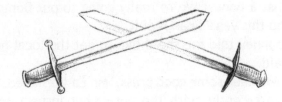

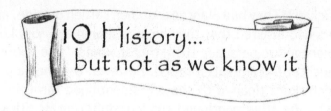

10 History...
but not as we know it

Over the next couple of weeks, the knights gained celebrity status throughout the school. Miss Loopney frequently came to shout '*marvellous*' at everything they did, and invite them for tea and crumpets in her office. Sir Gaseehad always blew her a kiss, which made her laugh like Star Wars, and flutter away down the corridor giggling.

The knights tried very hard not to pass wind in her presence, but one day, in assembly, Sir Trumpsalot got very agitated by a bee that was buzzing around his helmet trying to get in. In the midst of violent swiping and rather too-loud-for -assembly clashing of armour, he let out a very loud one!

PTTHHHHT!

He looked around, as if to say 'who was that?' then crashed out of the hall like a jumble of pots and pans falling out of a cupboard. Assembly dissolved into hysterical laughing.

Jack and Connor's classroom had been transformed. The walls were painted like large grey slabs of stone. And, at the top, near the ceiling, they were painted like castle ramparts. There was a big wooden banqueting table at the back of the room with modelling clay medieval food on it. Sir Gaseehad and Sir Windibot had tried to eat this, resulting in a slight case of the runs, and two days at home due to the after effects of 'extreme wind!'

Miss Shurry's class, 5S, had transformed their room into a medieval kitchen, with rushes (well, hay from a local farm) on the floor. They had a very realistic spit roast in the middle of the room, over a hearth built from bricks. (Shhhh! Don't tell

Mr. Stickler!) They had planted a kitchen garden outside, and the knights had insisted that they have real animals. Miss Loopney had managed to persuade them that it wouldn't be appropriate to slaughter the animals for food. However, they had a pig, and some chickens (loaned by the aforementioned farm) in a pen, made by the aforementioned and long-suffering Mr. Stickler.

The courtyard, in the middle of the school, had been transformed into the bailey, where the girls were encouraged to wander, dressed up in medieval gowns, playing medieval instruments made from all sorts of junk modelling materials. The boys had mock weapons training, with papier-mâché and plastic weapons, which the knights thought were truly ridiculous.

Even a cycling proficiency lesson was linked to medieval learning, as it was the perfect excuse for the knights to bring in their 'trusty steeds' and give the children a lesson in the importance of a horse to a knight. Sir Windibot had got used to Frillyfilly now, and seemed oblivious to the sniggers from the children.

'Percy is my pride and joy,' Sir Trumpsalot declared to the children on the playground, kitted out in their reflective gear and cycling helmets. 'And wearing the right clothing is essential to a knight. Thy 21st century versions of armour seem very appropriate to dealing with the hazards of modern riding. Cars are the most fearsome monsters I have ever come across. They are thy great enemy. Thou must protect thyselves from them at all costs.'

'**Always wear thine armour!**' Sir Gaseehad and Windibot shouted, like a battle cry. The children shouted it back and it turned into a chant.

Always wear thine armour!
Always wear thine armour!

'*Brilliant!*' the cycling proficiency officer said. 'I always have trouble getting them to wear this stuff!'

Miss Loopney and Mr. E. were in their element. The whole school had taken the knights to their hearts, and the children of year five were having an amazing time becoming experts in medieval life.

'It's time to get the Press in, Mr. E,' Miss Loopney said. 'Let's get Connor and Jack to introduce them to the knights, and show them round our *marvellous* medieval castle.'

The Press were impressed!

'Let's get a photo of the knights,' the journalist said. He organised them into a group. Jack and Connor stood in front of the knights. Miss Loopney nestled up to Sir Gaseehad. A few other children and Mr. E. bunched in at the sides. Sir Trumpsalot and Sir Windibot pulled suitable knightly poses.

'Is that a weapon in his hand?' Sir Trumpsalot asked Jack, as the journalist held up his camera.

'No, it's for taking pictures,' Jack said.

'Taking them where?'

Jack sighed. 'He points the camera at us and it makes a picture called a photograph. Then he downloads it to his computer and hey presto, it appears in the paper!'

'Forsooth! He is a wizard!'

'Yeah okay, he's a wizard!' It was easier than trying to explain.

Miss Loopney was hyper the next day. She pirouetted into Mr. E's classroom (which was quite a spectacular feat for a lady in high heels), crying, *'Marvellous! Just marvellous!'*

She wafted the newspaper in the air. 'Look, look my dears! Our lovely school is famous! I've had the council officials ringing up asking what we're doing here. Lots of other Heads want to come and look around! This is it! We've finally got them to see how *marvellous* this school is.'

At this point she leapt across to Jack's desk, picked him up in a huge bosomy embrace, and planted a big slobbery kiss on his cheek. 'Thank you so much for bringing the knights, my dear.'

The room erupted into laughter and cries of 'Urgh!' Then Sir Gaseehad (caught up in the moment) swept Miss Loopney off her high heels and kissed her, smackerooney, on the lips.

'Oh Sir Gaseehad!' she exclaimed, bursting forth into her famous laugh.

'Ha-ha-ha-haaaaa ha!'

'Let me carry thee back to thy solar, fair maiden,' he announced, and strode out of the room, blowing a trumpeting you-know-what behind him, with Miss Loopney tittering Star Wars hysterically.

Mr. E. got his football hooter out and the class calmed down. Maisey Bates did not cry!

'Time for medieval literacy. Over to Sir Trumpsalot!'

'Yay!' everyone shouted.

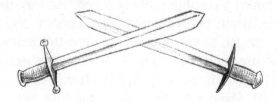

11 The Dragon is Coming

In the afternoon, as Sir Trumpsalot was passing Miss Loopney's office, he heard a terrible sobbing sound. He was about to rap on the door, when he overheard Miss Loopney cry, 'What are we going to do Mr. E? We've been dreading this moment for the last few months, and now it's here. After such a *marvellous* time yesterday, it is all to be spoilt. The Dragon is coming! I can't bear it!' She burst into loud wailing sobs again.

'Try not to worry too much, Miss L. Things have been so much better since the knights arrived. Maybe they will be our saving grace this time.'

Sir Trumpsalot drew back in horror. A dragon was coming? And it had terrorised Dempsey Road Primary before, by the sounds of it. He listened again, overhearing Miss Loopney wail, 'I'm going under, Mr. E.'

'No, no, don't think like that,' Mr. E. said. 'We'll be all right. We just need to keep our heads above water.'

Sir Trumpsalot was outraged. The knights would save the school! They would slay the dragon! He hurried off to find Sir Windibot and Sir Gaseehad.

Sir Gaseehad couldn't bear the thought of Miss Loopney's distress, and strode right into her office, followed by the other two.

He went down on bended knee and took the head teacher's hand in his. 'My dear Lady Loopney, we will defend Dempsey with our lives!' All three knights drew out their swords. Miss Loopney grabbed hold of Mr. E., letting out a small shriek.

'I overheard thee talking of a dragon, my lady. We are

accustomed to dragons and monsters of all kinds. Thou wilt never have to fear the monster again. Forsooth, we will deliver thee!' Sir Trumpsalot declared, gallantly.

'We are sworn to protect damsels in distress. This is thy castle, and we will not let it be taken!' proclaimed Sir Windibot, getting carried along in the moment.

'Oh, thank you, dear knights,' Miss Loopney said. 'If only you could deliver me from that dragon! Every visit seems worse than the last.'

'The heat just goes up and up,' Mr. E. added. 'People always say 'no smoke without fire' but this is a good school. We'd all like to run away at times, but we don't, because we love the children.'

'Verily, we must defend them. Never fear. We will make a plan,' Sir Trumpsalot said.

'You have certainly given us hope these past few weeks, Sir Trumpsalot,' Miss Loopney said, sniffing into her hanky.

'The children are buzzing,' Mr. E. added.

'Wherefore art they imitating bees?' Sir Windibot asked.

Sir Gaseehad groaned. 'They're not, Windi. The Great Myster-eeeeey means they are very enthusiastic since we came.'

'That's right,' Mr. E. said. 'Maybe this time it will be ok.'

*

At home, that evening, the knights sat around the kitchen table, with Jack and Connor. 'Miss Loopney saith that a dragon is coming to thy school. We must think of a plan to save the school,' said Sir Trumpsalot.

'A dragon?' Connor said, looking confused.

Sir Windibot answered. 'Aye! A fire breathing dragon. 'No smoke without fire,' she said.'

'And I think they are planning to dig a moat,' Sir Gaseehad said. 'Because Trumps heard them talking about going under and keeping their heads above water.'

'A moat would be a good place to start,' Sir Trumpsalot said.

'We shall help them!' cried Sir Gaseehad.

'I don't think they're seriously planning to dig a moat around the school,' Jack said.

'They must!' declared Sir Windibot.' What if the dragon brings troops? It has been known for dragons to command armies!'

'Sir Windi, we don't have dragons in the 21st century. I'm not sure what Miss Loopney was talking about, but it can't have been a real dragon,' Connor said.

'By my faith, it was! She was in deepest distress! And Mr. E. was not making any jokes!' Sir Trumpsalot said.

'Must be serious then,' said Connor.

'Well, whatever it is, you can save her,' Jack said.

Connor began, 'Yeah, all for one and one for ...'

'That's the three musketeers, Con,' Jack said.

'Begging your pardon?' Sir Gaseehad said.

'Never mind,' Jack said. 'But you guys are like King Arthur's Knights of the Round Table!'

'But we don't have a round table,' moaned Sir Windibot.

There was a pause. Jack looked at the kitchen table. It wasn't round and anyway these were not King Arthur's knights. They needed their own identity.

'Got it!' Jack shouted, wobbling the wonky kitchen table. 'You could be...... Knights of the Wobbly Table!'

Sir Gaseehad roared with laughter and high-fived Jack. 'Way-to-go, dude!'

Sir Trumpsalot nodded. 'By the Might of Mars! That is who we shall be.' He stood up, almost toppling the table. The other two rose abruptly too. They drew their swords and held them above their heads, touching the tips in a pyramid over the table.

'For the honour of Lady Loopney and Dempsey Road Primary!' Sir Gaseehad declared.

'Knights of the Wobbly Table!' they chorused.

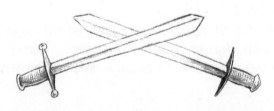

12 The Moat

In the middle of the night, a clanging began in the shed, followed by a lot of shushing. The knights emerged, carrying spades. They crept sort of quietly around the side of the house, and mounted their trusty steed bikes.

'Make haste, Percy!' Sir Trumpsalot whispered to his bike.

'Away, Lady Susan!' Sir Gaseehad hissed.

Sir Windibot stroked the tassels on his bike, 'No time to lose, my beauty.'

The knights arrived at Dempsey Road under the watchful eye of a large, crescent moon. The school was surrounded by a tall spiky fence and the gates were padlocked.

'At least they have some defences,' Sir Windibot said.

'Aye, but they obviously need more. Remember the dragon has terrorised them previously,' Sir Trumpsalot said. 'Start digging. We must have it done by morning.'

The knights dug and dug, in the fields surrounding the school. After a couple of hours, they had made only a little gully about three metres long and two metres deep.

'This is hopeless!' cried Sir Windibot.

'Be not in despair,' said Sir Trumpsalot. 'Keep digging!'

'He's right, Trumps,' Sir Gaseehad said. 'This is not getting us anywhere. We need more men.'

'But where will we find them at this ungodly hour?' Sir Windibot wailed.

Just then, Sir Trumpsalot spotted three men creeping along behind a wall, further down the street. 'There!' he cried. 'Those gentlemen appear to be on a mission. Perhaps they will help us.'

The three knights set off at speed, on their trusty steeds, towards the men.

'Prithee, stay!' shouted Sir Trumpsalot.

The men, wearing balaclavas and hoodies, looked up and froze, as the three knights, still partly dressed in armour (one riding a little girl's bike) screeched to a halt in front of them.

'Run for it!' one of the men shouted.

They tried to run away, but Sir Trumpsalot pedalled hard, overtaking them and doing a spectacular wheelie in front of them.

'Stay, knaves!' he commanded, as the other two knights brought up the rear.

The men were trapped.

'What ho, gentlemen! We are sorry to frighten thee, but wouldst thou be so kind as to give us thine assistance?'

The men looked at each other as if Sir Trumpsalot was speaking gobble-di-gook (which, of course, he was - to them!).

'Dempsey Road Primary needeth thy help,' Sir Trumpsalot said.

The men looked around, shiftily. Then one of them said, 'Ere, are you them knight blokes that've been 'elpin' out in school?'

'Aye, in truth, we are!' Sir Windibot said.

'He means, yes,' Sir Gaseehad translated.

'My kids go there,' another man said.

'And mine,' the third said.

'Excellent!' Sir Trumpsalot said. 'Then thou wilt surely want to help.'

'Er ... what exactly you doing then?' the first man said.

'We need to dig a moat around the school and we want to surprise Miss Loopney by having it done by morning,' Sir Gaseehad said.

The men looked at each other as if they were listening to three completely bonkers blokes.

'O -kay,' said one of them, slowly. 'My mate's got a digger on 'is drive, cos 'e's doing up 'is garden.'

'We need more than one digger,' Sir Windibot said (thinking they meant another man).

'Nah, this one'll 'ave it done in no time,' the man said.

*

The digger was noisy but, surprisingly, it didn't wake anyone. The knights were astounded by the monstrous machine. Sir Windibot wondered if he could borrow it to terrorise Sir Trumpsalot, in revenge for all the times he had set Rotateeth on him.

By 5 a.m. there was a moat (if only a small one) surrounding the school fence.

'Now we need water!' Sir Trumpsalot said.

'No problem mate,' one of the men said. In a short while he and his friends were back with a large hose. 'Now, keep it under yer 'at, but this is comin' off the waterboard supply; direct.'

'Well, it's government business this, innit?' said another. The men agreed and the knights didn't argue. The moat filled up.

At 7 a.m. the knights admired their handiwork, shook hands with their hooded helpers, and went home to the shed for a well-deserved rest.

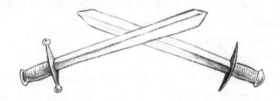

13 Surprise!

When Miss Loopney drove up to the school gates at 7.40, she had to do an emergency stop. Her eyes bulged out of her skull as she clapped her hand to her mouth and let out a blood-curdling shriek.

AAAAAGGHH!

Fumbling her mobile out of her handbag, she called Mr. E.

'Mr. E., *Mr. E.*, you're notgonnabeeelieveeethis! Abigditch! Alllairooondeeschool! whaaaterwegonnadooo!!!'

'Miss Loopney, slow down, you're not making any sense!' Mr. E. said.

'Get down here now!' She managed, before flinging herself across the steering wheel and wailing.

When Mr. E. arrived he was dumbstruck. 'Who could have ....? What on earth.....? Wait a minute ....'

'What?' Miss Loopney asked.

'Does this look like a moat to you?'

'Well .... I .... Yes, in fact it does,' Miss Loopney said.

More of the staff were arriving now. 'At least they've left us a kind of drawbridge to drive over,' said a Year 4 teacher.

'You don't think ...?' Miss Loopney said. 'The knights!'

*

When Connor and Jack arrived, at a quarter to nine, there was a crowd of children and parents staring in amazement at the moat, and gossiping wildly. Miss Loopney was standing on the drive. She was wearing her yes-of-course-this-was-all-planned head teacher face, with the larger than life smile.

'Isn't our new moat exciting, everyone? It's all part of our *marvellous* medieval extravaganza! We are making it as authentic as possible! Now, come in my dears, come in. Cross the drawbridge.' With that she gave an exaggerated Star Wars laugh,'*Ha-ha-ha-haaaaaaaaaa ha!*' and ushered the children along the drive and into school.

'What's going on, Mr. E?' Jack asked, when they were all settled in their medieval castle classroom.

'I'd have thought *you* could tell ME that, Jack,' Mr. E. said, looking rather sterner than Jack liked him to.

'What do you mean, Mr. E?'

Mr. E. gave Jack one of his wiggly eyebrow stares, which means: *I-think-you-DO-know-what-I-mean-and-you'd-better-tell-me-right-now!*

Jack squirmed a little; then it dawned on him. 'Oh ... you think the knights ...'

'Come on Jack,' Mr. E. said. 'Of course the knights did it. Although I don't know how! Do you mean to tell me you didn't know anything about it?'

'I didn't. Honest.' Jack said. 'Well, I did know that they wanted to help Miss Loopney fight a dragon. But I don't know what that's all about.'

'A dragon!' Alex piped up. 'Cool!'

'A dragon?' Mr. E. said. 'But that's ridicu..... *Ohhhhhh*, that dragon!' All of a sudden Mr. E. remembered his conversation with Miss Loopney. 'It'll take more than a moat to keep her out!'

'So there is a *real* dragon?' Connor asked. The whole class were listening now.

'Oh yes,' Mr. E. nodded his head thoughtfully. 'There certainly is!'

'Don't be daft Mr. E.,' James said. 'There's no such things.'

'Ha!' Mr. E. wagged his finger. 'That's what *you* think!'

He grabbed the sweeping brush, from the corner, and jumped

up on the desk. He held the brush between his legs, and galloped over the tables to the back of the room, accompanied by shrieks of laughter, and cheers from the children.

'Once, long ago,' he cried, in his deep, dramatic, story-telling voice, 'there lived dragons! Huge fire-breathing creatures, with scales and spikes and teeth sharp enough to open a tin of tuna in one go, *without a ring-pull!*'

(Weird looks all around!)

'Dragons roamed the earth, devouring men and capturing damsels in distress. No not *DIS* dress,' (he mimicked wearing a dress) 'dis-*STRESS*. (I always wanted to do that joke.)'

He galloped to the front of the classroom on his broom horse. 'Anyway, dragons roamed the countryside, terrorizing the people. Especially *children!*'

Maisey Bates' screamed! 'Not you, Maisey,' Mr. E. said, quickly. 'But...' he held up the broom, like a sword, *'Buuuuut,'* he said again, lingering on the word for dramatic effect, 'help was at hand, in the form of brave knights like Sir Trumpsalot, Sir Gaseehad and Sir Windibot.'

'YAY!' everyone cheered.

'And *now*,' Mr. E. paused for more dramatic effect, 'A new and greater terror lurks; waiting to devour Dempsey Road Primary. A great and fearsome dragon is prowling near to our school, *as we speak!*'

(Gasps all round.)

At this point Maisey Bates lost it, and was about to flee the classroom.

'Stop, Maisey!' Mr. E. shouted, pointing the broom at her. She was so shocked, that she froze, mid-wail! 'We need each and every person to be brave. We can defeat the dragon! With the help of ...'

'The Knights of the Wobbly Table!' Sir Gaseehad shouted, bursting into the room. The knights had been watching from the door as Mr. E. gave his speech.

Mr. E. stared at Sir Gaseehad, in slight confusion, then carried on. 'With the help of the Knights of the... Wobbly Table? We will have victory over the dragon!' He held the broom over his head, and shook it up and down. The whole class and the knights erupted into shouts and cheers, and began running around the room hysterically. Even Maisey Bates, tears streaking her cheeks, began to laugh! The knights trumped loudly and didn't even care!

'Oh my giddy goodness! What is going on here!' cried Miss Loopney, coming into the room. At first, no one heard her, until she picked up Mr. E.'s football hooter, and blasted everyone with it.

PARP!

'Ouch! That's loud,' Mr. E. said.

'The Great Myster-eeeeey was just giving a rousing speech,' Sir Windibot said.

'About fighting the dragon,' Connor said.

Miss Loopney was rarely cross, but this was one of those rare occasions. 'Mr. E.! A word!'

She marched out of the room, Mr. E. trailing shamefacedly behind her.

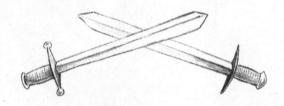

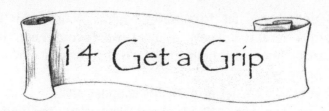

14 Get a Grip

'Mr. E. we have to get a grip! I've had the letter! The Ramsbottom woman will be here on Friday. We have two days to prepare the school for inspection, and your class are running round like fanatical football fans, whose team have just won the FA cup!'

'Sorry about that,' Mr. E. mumbled.

Miss Loopney waved away his comment. 'Never mind. We need a plan to make sure we get a good inspection. Another bad one, and it's down the drain for Dempsey. I'm calling an emergency staff meeting straight after school. And get those knights and Jack Sanders in here now. I want to know what-the-blueberries they thought they were doing, digging a whopping great ditch round our school.'

Jack was very worried. He had never seen Miss Loopney in such a state. The knights were very quiet. They didn't like to upset the head teacher. In stressful situations, it was hard for them to keep the curse from embarrassing them. Sir Windibot had to keep excusing himself and run down the corridor to the toilet! But they could still hear him from the office. Sir Trumpsalot and Sir Gaseehad only just managed to keep control of their cursed bottoms!

Miss Loopney stood with her hands on her hips. Her face was pinched, and her eyebrows looked like two skinny caterpillars having an argument, as she scrunched up her forehead. Jack cowered behind the knights.

'What made you think digging a big ditch around the school was a good idea?'

'My dear Lady,' Sir Trumpsalot began, 'A dragon is a very dangerous threat! I know a moat would not keep it out, necessarily, but it will help to defend thee against any army it might bring.'

'What dragon? What army?' Miss Loopney said.

'The dragon you talked about yesterday, my Lady,' Sir Gaseehad said.

Miss Loopney turned pale, and slumped backwards into her chair. Sir Gaseehad knelt, and grabbed her hand. 'Sweet lady, art thou unwell?'

'That *DRAGON* is not the kind of dragon you are thinking of. She is a horrible, nasty, mean, fault-finding, criticizing, cruel....' Miss Loopney burst into wailing tears.

'Boo hoooooooo! Boo hoo hoo hoooooooo!'

'Dear Lady Loopney!' Sir Gaseehad soothed. 'Fear not. We will protect thee!'

Miss Loopney pulled out her frilly handkerchief, and blew her nose. 'She is coming on Friday, and this is our last chance. If we fail, *WE ARE FINISHED!*'

'My Lady, I beseech thee, do not cry. We will save thee,' Sir Trumpsalot said, as Sir Gaseehad tried to wipe Miss Loopney's face with a blue paper towel. She pushed him aside.

'How? How? And *HOW* am I going to explain a huge ditch around the school?'

Jack crept out from behind Sir Trumpsalot. 'Miss Loopney, maybe the knights could really save us. Maybe we could say we've arranged a medieval extravaganza for the inspector and the moat is just part of it.'

Miss Loopney sniffed. 'I suppose it's worth a try. Nothing else has worked with the abominable woman.'

'Never fear, my lady,' Sir Gaseehad said, kissing Miss Loopney's hand. 'The Knights of the Wobbly Table are going to save thee from this dragon!'

'Oh, Sir Gaseehad, you are our last hope,' Miss Loopney said, smiling weakly.

*

That evening, the knights, Jack and Connor sat around the wobbly table making plans for the inspection day. Jack had made a mind map of ideas. Some classes could do jousting, others medieval music. A sword-fighting display and a medieval banquet were also planned. But the knights still didn't really seem to understand that the dragon was not really a dragon. They had conjured up an image of a dragon in disguise, and still thought that they were going to have to slay it. This was rather worrying Jack and Connor.

'We just need to make the dragon happy,' Jack tried to explain.

'Why?' asked Sir Windibot. 'Surely thou wouldst defeat thine enemy?'

'The teachers just need a good report,' Connor said.

'Ah, like in the newspaper,' Sir Trumpsalot said. 'The newspaper could report the defeat of the Dragon!'

'No, no,' Jack said. 'You don't get it.'

'Get what?' Sir Windibot said.

The boys looked to Sir Gaseehad to explain, but even he didn't 'get it.'

'We will train the boys well tomorrow,' Sir Trumpsalot said. 'Lady Loopney and the other ladies can lead the girls in music and preparing the banquet.'

'Well, that sounds safe enough,' Jack said to Connor, hoping that it would be.

'How are you getting on?' Mum asked, coming into the kitchen. 'Do you want any more snacks?'

'Snakes? Where?' Sir Windibot cried, jumping up and pulling out his sword.

Jack and Connor groaned and began banging their heads on the table.

'No Windi,' Sir Gaseehad said. 'Snacks are food, remember?'

Sir Trumpsalot turned to Mum. 'Dear lady, we are fully replenished, thank you kindly.'

'He means 'we're full, thanks, Mum!" Jack said.

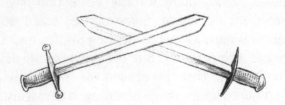

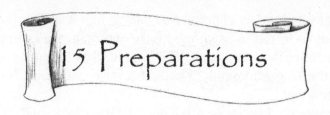

15 Preparations

On Thursday, the school was a bubbling cauldron of activity. All the children had taken home letters about the inspection and the medieval extravaganza. Many children brought in bikes with labels around them, naming their 'trusty steeds.' Sir Trumpsalot was giving them a horse-bike riding lesson around the playground. Under his instruction, some teachers and children were setting up a jousting arena.

'We need lances for the jousting,' he said to Mr. E.

'Oh ha ha!' Mr. E. laughed, nervously. 'I don't think that will be allowed, Sir Trumps. 'Mr. Stickler will be onto you!'

'We could make some pretend lances Mr. E.,' Jack said. 'Tin foil and lots of wrapping paper tubes.'

'Erm ... I really don't think...'

'Mr. E., we have to impress the inspector,' Connor persisted.

'Ok,' Mr. E. agreed, nervously.

Miss Loopney had cheered up since yesterday, and was busy throwing herself into banquet preparations. A huge pan of pottage was on the boil, made with beans and leeks. The knights were strictly forbidden to eat it, as everyone knew the rhyme:

'Beans, beans, good for your heart, the more you eat the more you ...'

Miss Loopney was determined there would be as little of that as possible.

A spit roast was going to be cooked on the day of the visit. There was no way the new school pig was going to be roasted though, despite the knights' protests that this is what the animal was for. The children had named him Rollie, as he loved to wallow in the massive mud patch he had made, especially when he had an audience. Fortunately, Miss Loopney agreed with the children, and had bought a huge pork joint from the supermarket.

She planned to serve a banquet in the dining hall at lunch time, and invite the inspector to it. There would be a fish dish and cold meats from the school kitchen, as well as the spit roast and the pottage. The children would drink milk and water and there would be a little wine for the teachers and inspector. She had been up all night shopping on the internet (and paying a fortune for next-day delivery) to provide some wonderful medieval tankards and goblets, as well as wooden bowls to eat from.

Sword-fighting (or weapons training, according to the knights) was being rehearsed under the very controlled discipline of the knights. There were home-made maces, poleaxes, flails, clubs and cudgels, as well as an assortment of swords. Mr. E. however, had put his foot down when two boys appeared with home-made crossbows! He had swiftly confiscated them when Sir Windibot had suggested they try target practice, shooting apples off each other's heads!

The boys were having a whale of a time! 'This is amazing!' Alex shouted at Jack, as he thrust his sword forwards and Jack twisted out of the way.

'I know. I'm so glad the knights landed in my shed,' Jack replied, swiping his sword at Alex's head.

Alex ducked and thrust another jab at Jack. 'Landed in your shed? What do you mean?'

Jack had forgotten that the knights were meant to be a travelling theatre group. He laughed, trying to think of a cover story. 'I meant that they're staying in the shed 'cos we don't have enough rooms in our house. They've come a long way to do this project.'

Sir Gaseehad commanded all the boys to stop, and put their swords down. Alex gave Jack a friendly thump. 'Well, this is the best school project I've ever done!'

The girls were learning medieval songs, and Miss Loopney had managed to source some musicians to come and show how to play lutes, dulcimers, psalteries and tabors. Some children were rehearsing a play about ordinary life in medieval times, while others were preparing to show off the research they had done, and read stories about the times. While the knights had been around, some wonderful displays and photographs about the children's learning had gone up on the walls. All the children were going to arrive in medieval costumes tomorrow. Everything was ready.

'I think this could go well for us, Miss Loopney,' Mr. E. said that evening, when all the children had gone home. 'If she's not pleased by this I don't know what will impress her.'

'Oh dear, I hope she is Mr. E. And I just hope those knights behave themselves and keep their 'little problem' under control.'

'Maybe Sir Gaseehad could woo her and sweep her off her feet,' Mr. E. said, chuckling.

Miss Loopney gave him one of her stern looks. 'I truly hope not, Mr. E.! That would be a disaster.'

Mr. E. nodded seriously, but thought he saw a hint of jealousy in her eyes.

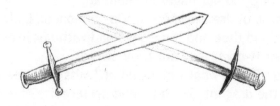

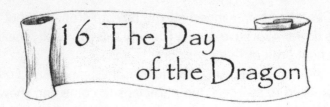

16 The Day of the Dragon

The next morning, the knights woke very early to prepare for battle. They had polished their armour and sharpened their swords the night before. Jack was woken by battle shouts, and louder than usual clanking of armour, as well as the normal round of loud trumping, coming from the shed.

The knights arrived at school, before seven o'clock, to find Miss Loopney and most of the teachers already there. Miss Loopney was coming out of her office in a flurry of paperwork. Sir Gaseehad strode into the school, dramatically kneeling before her and kissing her hand.

'Chill out, My Lady! We are here to protect thee. Be not afraid!'

Miss Loopney couldn't help but be flattered by Sir Gaseehad's attentions. 'Oh, oh Sir Gaseehad, really! Oh my!' She blushed all over her rosy cheeks, and gave a little Star Wars giggle, despite the churning in her stomach.

Recovering herself, she put on her I'm-in-charge voice, saying, 'Now, just you behave yourself Sir Gaseehad, and you two!' She waggled her finger at them all.

Sir Trumpsalot drew his sword, 'On our honour, Lady Loopney! We will defend thee and Dempsey Road with our lives!'

The other two whisked out their swords.

'Oh dear! That's what I'm afraid of,' Miss Loopney said.

'Fie on the dragon!' Sir Gaseehad declared.

'By the Might of Mars, that beast shall be slain!' Sir Windibot shouted.

'But ...' Miss Loopney tried to interrupt the drama.

'There is no time to lose,' Sir Windibot said. 'We must make final preparations for the attack.'

'It's not an attack,' Miss Loopney tried again, but the knights swept away down the corridor without listening. The head teacher flopped into her chair and groaned.

*

'Once the children are inside we must make a barricade,' Sir Trumpsalot said. 'Despite our moat, the defences of this castle are somewhat inadequate.'

'Then we must gather the swordsmen together, and send all the women and children into the bailey, as it is the safest place in the castle,' Sir Windibot said.

'I will hasten to the kitchen and prepare boiling oil to pour from the ramparts,' Sir Gaseehad said.

Meanwhile, Jack and Connor were walking to school, dressed in armour made mainly from reams of tin foil and cardboard.

'What if the knights attack the inspector?' Connor said.

'The school could be in even worse trouble, and it would all be my fault,' said Jack. 'We have to stop them.'

Connor shook his head. 'But how? They don't understand, and it's all got really crazy!'

'We'll have to protect the inspector from them somehow,' Jack said.

'But we can't follow her around all day,' Connor protested.

'We could, if Mr. E. is in on it,' said Jack. 'He'll understand. He doesn't want the school to get a bad report. Let's tell him the plan when we get to school.'

*

The children arrived at 8.40 dressed in medieval clothes. There were peasants, rich gentlemen, ladies and, of course, lots of knights. Mr. E. had hired a special costume from a shop, and looked like a character from a Shakespeare play in his hose

(tights for men!) and doublet. Everyone was buzzing with the excitement of all the activities that lay ahead for the day. They had almost forgotten that the inspector was coming.

Miss Loopney called an assembly. She was jittery because she didn't know at what point the inspector would arrive. However, she put on her head teacher I'm-not-afraid-of-anything smile.

'Good morning everyone.'

'Good morrrrrrning Miss Loopney. Good morrrrrrrrning ev'-ry-bo-dy!' The children chorused.

'What a *marvellous* day we have planned. It will be

the highlight of our medieval project. Our thanks go to the knights ...'

At this point a roaring cheer went up throughout the hall, and before Miss Loopney could say another word, Sir Trumpsalot stepped forward.

'Thank you, Lady Loopney. I shall take over from here. We have a battle strategy to work out for the day ahead. We must be ready for the dragon's attack.'

At this point, some of the younger children gasped, and began to whisper to one another.

Miss Loopney tried to butt in. 'Don't worry my dears, there's no dragon!'

But Sir Trumpsalot carried on. 'Dragons are dangerous and cunning. We must be on our guard. Sometimes they disguise themselves, in order to get into our midst, and I fear that this is what is happening today!'

Some of the younger children looked tearful and the noise level began to rise. Teachers bent forward to comfort the little ones.

Miss Loopney tried to interrupt again, but Sir Gaseehad stepped in, putting his arm around her and drawing her to one side, despite her protests.

Mr. E. stood up to try and take control, but, at the same moment, Sir Trumpsalot flung out his arms and knocked Mr. E. to the floor.

Oof!

Gasps and giggles flew around the room.

'DO NOT BE AFRAID! Thou art safe in our hands,' Sir Trumpsalot proclaimed.

'Mr. E. wasn't!' Connor whispered to Jack.

'We will defend thee and thou wilt help us to defeat the dragon. Never more shall it terrorize Dempsey Road!'

A massive cheer went up from the year 5 and 6 children, which rippled down through the ranks, until everyone was happy again. Some teachers stood up, bamboozled, not quite sure what to do. Mr. E. rubbed his nose.

Miss Loopney looked like she was about to burst into tears, but she cleared her throat, stuck on her I'm-still-not-afraid-of-anything smile and said, in an ever so slightly trembling voice, 'Back to class everyone. Have a *marvellous* day!'

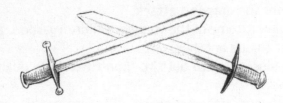

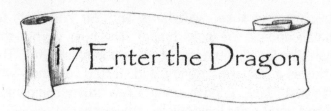

17 Enter the Dragon

Sir Gaseehad barged in to Mr. E.'s classroom. 'What ho! Listen up dudes!'

Jack and Connor exchanged eye-rolling, at Sir Gaseehad's attempts to be '21st century.'

'All women and girls, with Miss Cuticle to the bailey. Men and boys; follow me!'

'Now, just a minute, Sir Gassy,' Mr. E. said (quite sternly for him) 'Is this a command from Miss Loopney?'

Sir Gaseehad gave a big bellowing laugh. 'Oh, Great Myster-eeeey! We are in command here. A woman could never be in charge of a siege situation.' He turned to the class. 'Now, follow me! And bring thy chairs and tables.' Then back to Mr. E. 'Like the outfit, by the way, Great Myster-eeeey. Cool!'

Before Mr. E. could stop them, the boys were up and dragging furniture after Sir Gaseehad. Mr. E. tried his hooter but no one was paying any attention. Even Maisey Bates was already moving towards the door.

'Well,' Mr. E. sighed, 'If you can't beat 'em, join 'em! Girls, off to the bailey with Miss Cuticle.'

*

Outside the front of the school, the knights, and most of the older boys, were building a barricade with the furniture. Miss Loopney was nowhere to be seen. She had taken one look at the whole thing and retreated to her office, crying, 'We're doomed! *Doomed!*'

Sir Trumpsalot was in command.

'Now, most of thee, wait here, with Sir Windibot, for the dragon to appear. Weapons ready!' The boys gave a shout of triumph! And Sir Windibot let out a loud you-know-what. The boys took this as a sort of battle cry, and started you-know-whatting themselves! 'Jack, Connor, bring a few trusty companions. Sir Gaseehad and I need look-outs on the ramparts!'

The knights had borrowed a ladder from Mr. Stickler's shed, and propped it against the side of the school, up to the lowest part of the roof. Connor, Jack and three other boys climbed up behind them. Clambering up to the next level, they made their way to the front of the school. Down below they could see the rest of the boys and Sir Windibot, poised, ready for action behind the barricade. All the you-know-whatting had stopped and a menacing silence had taken its place.

'This is so cool!' Jack said.

'Yeah!' Connor replied, although he did keep well away from the edge.

The knights began scanning the skies for signs of the dragon, and scanning the horizon for signs of an advancing army. The boys copied them. Behind Sir Gaseehad were several large pans of ... something!

'At least we'll be able to keep an eye on the knights up here,' Jack whispered. 'I don't like the look of those big pans.'

The knights patrolled impatiently around the roof-ramparts.

'There!' shouted Jack, all of a sudden.

A shiny red mini was making its way up Dempsey Road.

'Where? What?' Sir Trumpsalot said.

'There, that car,' Jack said. 'That's got to be her!'

'It has armour!' Sir Gaseehad cried. 'Not only is the dragon in disguise as a weak and defenceless woman, but it has an armoured steed.'

'A car, Sir Gassy. You've seen loads of them,' Connor said.

'God's blood! This is indeed a cunning creature!' Sir Gaseehad said.

'But it does not appear to have brought an army,' Sir Trumpsalot said.

'It must be powerful,' Sir Gaseehad shouted down to the troops below. 'Prepare for battle!'

The boys and Sir Windibot gave another rousing shout, and let off a few battle trumps for good measure.

The car pulled up to the school gates and a bemused woman got out. She was tall and thin, with rectangular glasses balanced on the tip of her long nose. Her bony shoulder blades stuck out of her dark suit.

'See those shoulders?' Sir Trumpsalot said to Jack, 'She's got

wings folded underneath there.'

'Don't be silly,' Jack said, but he did stare more closely.

The inspector scowled at the gates, padlocked by the knights; then she noticed the moat, and the children awaiting her behind the barricade.

'What is the meaning of this!' she declared. 'Let me in at once!'

At that moment Miss Loopney ran out of the front door, almost tripping over several boys in armour, and hurried towards the gates. She was followed by Mr. E. and Mr. Stickler carrying a large pair of bolt cutters.

'Mrs. Ramsbottom!' she declared, in a slightly hysterical voice. 'We have been so looking forward to your visit! This is Mr. Eades.'

Mr. E. put his hand through the gates, to shake the inspector's, but she folded her arms across her chest.

'We're studying medieval times this term, and today is our medieval enactment day,' Mr. E. said. 'The children have got somewhat carried away with their recreation of a fortified castle. But, never fear, Mr. Stickler will have you in here in no time.'

At this point Miss Loopney gave a VERY high pitched Star Wars laugh.

Ha-Ha-Ha Haaaaaaa-Ha!

Mr. Stickler began to cut the padlock off the gates. 'Friend or foe?' she said, trying to make a joke.

But Mrs. Ramsbottom was so not amused that her face looked like a squished strawberry that has been chewed up, spat out and trampled on!

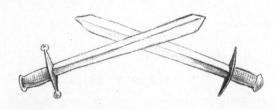

18 Boiling Oil

The gates were finally opened, and Mrs. Ramsbottom drove her car into the space specially marked (last night by Mr. Stickler): VIP - Very Important Person.

Or as Mr. Stickler had called it, 'Very Infuriating Person.'

As Mrs. Ramsbottom approached the building, clipboard and laptop in hand, Sir Windibot and the boys began to roar.

'Get ready!' Sir Trumpsalot cried, from the ramparts.

'Get the pans of boiling oil ready,' Sir Gaseehad shouted to the boys on the roof.

'The what?' Jack said.

'Well, it is meant to be boiling oil but I couldn't get that, so the cook gave me this.' He opened the lids and the smell of hot chocolate hit the boy's nostrils.

'*Mmmmmmm,*' Connor said.

'We pour this on the enemy to try and stop her,' said Sir Gaseehad.

'We can't!' Jack shouted.

'We *must!*' Sir Trumpsalot said.

'But ... but what about Miss Loopney. You might get her!'

'Gadzooks! Jack has a point! We cannot risk hitting Lady Loopney. The dragon seems to have her under its spell! She is leading it into the castle.'

As Mrs. Ramsbottom approached the roaring boys, fear flickered in her eyes. Mr. E. thought about using his hooter, but decided it might be taken as a signal to attack. Miss Loopney knew she wouldn't stand a chance of getting them to be quiet.

She gave a little Star Wars laugh. 'It's all part of the act,

Mrs. Ramsbottom. This is how medieval knights would defend their castle. We even have some actors with us who have been inspiring the children over the last few weeks.'

The inspector scowled even harder.

Miss Loopney managed to steer her through the ranks. 'Hold fire, young knights. We come in peace.' She pulled out a white handkerchief from her sleeve and waved it in the air.

'Hold fire!' Sir Windibot commanded.

Breathing a small sigh of relief, Miss Loopney held the door open for the inspector. However, at that very moment, one of the boys on the roof tipped up a large pan of the hot chocolate.

'**Nooooo!**' Jack shouted.

(The next bit seemed to happen in slow motion, as it does in all good action movies!)

Mr. E., who was following the inspector, glanced up to see it heading straight for her. He dived, pushing her through the door, just before the deluge of hot chocolate drenched him. The boys howled with laughter.

(Just in case you are the type of person who is concerned with health and safety, the hot chocolate was more lukewarm than hot. Mr. E. was unharmed.)

Miss Loopney looked up, in horror. 'Get down from there!' she screeched, as Sir Gaseehad, Sir Trumpsalot and the boys peered over the edge.

She took one look at the chocolate-coated Mr. E. and hissed, 'Round the back! Get changed quickly! And deal with them!' Then she scuttled inside after the inspector.

Mrs. Ramsbottom was furious! 'What does that man think he is doing? How dare he shove me! What is going on out there?'

Miss Loopney ushered Mrs. Ramsbottom into her office. 'Very sorry, Mrs. Ramsbottom, I think he tripped. He's just gone to set up another activity. Isn't this fun?' She took the inspector by the arm, calling out over her shoulder, 'Mrs. Diamond – cups of coffee in my office, *NOW*... Please!'

Mr. E. found the ladder propped up around the back of the school. 'Get down here at once!' he shouted up.

The boys had never seen him so mad. Even though hot chocolate dripped from his hair and medieval clothes, they were not even tempted to laugh.

'Mr. E., we tried to stop them,' Jack said.

'We really did,' Connor chipped in, 'but they got carried away. Even Sir Gaseehad had called off the attack!'

Mr. E. looked at them with his hands on his hips. No one messed with Mr. E. when he occasionally got angry.

Sir Trumpsalot and Sir Gaseehad were very embarrassed. 'Oh Great Myster-eeeeey,' Sir Gaseehad said, kneeling before him, 'We are most humbly contrite and totally sorry, dude.'

'We are indeed most distraught at this misadventure,' Sir Trumpsalot said.

In their embarrassment it was impossible for the knights to keep control of their curse and a lot of loud trumping noises followed. The boys began to giggle.

'Sorry dudes,' said Sir Gaseehad.

'We are deeply distressed at this wretched curse,' Sir Trumpsalot cried.

'Never mind that,' Mr. E. said. 'Start preparations for the jousting demonstration. And get control of your .... bottoms!'

'Right away, Great Myster-eeeeey! Of course!' Sir Trumpsalot said.

Mr. E. trudged away, to get changed, dripping a trail of hot chocolate behind him.

'And remember, it is just acting. Not for real!' he shouted over his shoulder.

'What does he mean, not real?' Sir Trumpsalot said.

'Forsooth! This could be our chance to catch the dragon off guard. Then one of us could spear her with a jousting lance,' Sir Gaseehad said.

Jack and Connor looked at each other in dismay.

19 Jousting

'I really need to see all your documents, Miss Loopney,' Mrs. Ramsbottom said, sipping a cup of coffee and nibbling at the most expensive chocolate biscuits Mrs. Diamond had been able to buy. 'This is a very serious inspection, and I intend to be thorough.'

'Of course, of course,' Miss Loopney said, smiling like a crazy woman, while her stomach did somersaults. 'And that is why we are thrilled that you have come on our *marvellous* medieval day. You couldn't have chosen a better day to see this school at it's creative best.'

'Hmmm,' was all the inspector said.

'We pride ourselves on giving the children a realistic experience of history in this school. And the theatre group have been providing the children with such a *marvellous* opportunity. We've covered all aspects of the curriculum through our medieval topic.'

'Indeed!' said the inspector, glancing over the top of her glasses, as she shuffled papers from her briefcase.

At that moment, Mrs. Diamond knocked on the door and peered in, nervously. 'The children are ready for you, out on the playground, Miss Loopney.'

'Are they?' she said, looking at Mrs. Diamond for some clue as to what was going on. Mrs. Diamond just shrugged her shoulders, whilst keeping a fixed grin firmly in place.

'They are! Yes!' Miss Loopney said, in her head teacher of-course-I-know-what's-going-on voice.

Mrs. Ramsbottom raised her eyebrows in a '*Welllllll?*' type of way.

'Shall we go to the playground?' Miss Loopney said, trying not to look as worried as she felt.

In the playground things looked calm and well organised. Two rows of chairs had been placed along either edge, where teachers and children, dressed in their medieval clothing, sat waiting. Running down the middle of the two rows was a fence made out of hurdles. This was the jousting gauntlet. The hired musicians played their instruments. And, on the right hand side, the bike shelter had been transformed into a royal box, decorated with flowers and ribbons.

A flicker of a smile twitched on the inspector's lips.

Sir Gaseehad approached Miss Loopney and the dragon.

'My Lady,' he said taking Miss Loopney's hand, 'May I escort you and your 'guest' to the royal box, to behold the jousting tournament?'

Miss Loopney gave a light Star Wars giggle as Sir Gaseehad kissed her hand and led them to seats in the decorated bike shed.

When they were seated, two boys, dressed as knights, were escorted by Sir Windibot and Sir Trumpsalot to opposite ends of the jousting gauntlet. They were both riding bikes and carrying home-made lances. Their faces were hidden by their armour.

Mr. E. stood up. 'Let the jousting begin!' He gave a sharp blast on his hooter and a loud cheer went up.

The boys began racing towards each other on their bikes at an alarming speed. They held out their lances in front of them with one hand, the other on the handlebars. Miss Loopney covered her eyes!

There was an almighty crash as the hurdles flew everywhere and the boys ended up in a big heap. Mr. E. and some other teachers ran to pick them up. 'No harm done!' Mr. E. shouted. 'It's all very controlled and staged!'

'Is no one dead?' Sir Trumpsalot asked, looking in the direction of the dragon.

'No, Sir Trumps! Thankfully!' Mr. E. said, picking up the dazed boys.

'Disappointing,' Sir Trumpsalot said. 'Next competitors!'

This time it was Sir Windibot and Sir Gaseehad who took to the gauntlet.

Mr. E. looked worried, but he didn't know what else to do, so he sounded his hooter. The children were screaming with excitement for the knight they wanted to win.

'Fear not,' Sir Trumpsalot shouted to Mr. E. 'They have a plan.'

Mr. E. groaned.

The two knights sped towards each other on their trusty bike-steeds. Suddenly, Sir Windibot veered away from the gauntlet, and towards the bike-shed/royal box. A demon driver on his faithful, pink, tasselled Frillyfilly, his knees almost knocked him out as he pedalled furiously.

Miss Loopney panicked as she realised he was heading straight for them. Mrs. Ramsbottom was paralysed with fear.

'Abandon bike-shed!' cried Miss Loopney.

Both women leapt head first out of the bike shed, as Sir Windibot gave a startling battle cry and bounced spectacularly off the inside of the perspex.

Sir Gaseehad rushed to pick up Miss Loopney. Meanwhile, the inspector lay motionless on the other side of the shed.

We did it! Sir Trumpsalot declared. 'The dragon is dead!'

A hush fell over the playground, as everyone watched to see if the inspector would move.

After what seemed forever, she sat up, her glasses mangled across her nose, her suit covered in dirt. She looked around her, as if she couldn't quite remember where she was. Then, she knelt up on her hands and knees, her bony shoulder blades sticking out even more. No one moved.

'God's teeth! It still lives!' Sir Gaseehad said.

'And look, it is about to flex its wings and reveal it's true identity!' Sir Trumpsalot shouted. 'Take cover, everyone. *Run for your lives!*'

Mass panic broke out. Children ran around the playground screaming and crying. The teachers tried to herd them inside, while Miss Loopney pushed Sir Gaseehad aside and, got up to help the inspector.

But she was stopped in her tracks. Someone else had got to Mrs. Ramsbottom first.

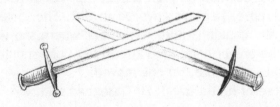

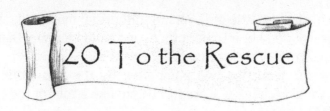

20 To the Rescue

'Can I help you?' said Maisey Bates, bending down and offering the inspector her hand.

Mrs. Ramsbottom couldn't speak. Her face was white, and her mouth kept flapping open and shut, like a gormless goldfish.

'Don't be frightened,' Maisey said. 'I'm normally frightened of everything, but, since the knights have been here, I've got very brave.'

The inspector looked at the girl curiously. Maisey put out her hand and Mrs. Ramsbottom took it. The girl led the inspector to a chair and sat her down. 'Do you need some water?'

The inspector nodded.

'I'll just go and get you some.'

As Maisey walked away, Miss Loopney approached the inspector with caution. 'Mrs. Ramsbottom, are you hurt? Oh dear, oh dear. Let's get you to my office.'

The inspector allowed Miss Loopney to guide her into the school. She still couldn't speak. They met Maisey coming out with a glass of water.

Miss Loopney quickly took the glass from her and handed it to Mrs. Ramsbottom. 'Well done Maisey,' she said, smiling at the girl.

Maisey smiled at the inspector.

'Thank you,' Mrs. Ramsbottom croaked.

Miss Loopney ushered the inspector towards her office. 'Let's get you cleaned up,' she said. 'Oh dear, such enthusiasm! The children got a little carried away with their jousting. However, we have lots of other things to show you.'

'Such a lovely little girl,' Mrs. Ramsbottom muttered, as Miss Loopney guided her into her office, and called for Mrs. Diamond to help soothe and clean up the inspector.

After much fussing and pampering by the two ladies, the inspector gradually recovered. 'I would like a tour of the school now, Miss Loopney.'

'Of course, Mrs. Ramsbottom. Right now?'

'Yes. I need to see what goes on in the classrooms.'

Miss Loopney swallowed hard, and gave her high-pitched Star Wars laugh to disguise the rising panic in her voice. What would the knights have in store next?

She guided the inspector through the Key Stage One classrooms without any problem. The children were busy with role play (knights mixed with fire fighters and nurses). They were also making medieval food out of playdough. Some children read very nicely to the inspector, and Miss Loopney thought she saw her smile at one point.

'Well done,' she whispered to one of the teachers.

In lower Key Stage Two, children were writing reports on the joust.

These are for our medieval newspaper,' a boy told the inspector.

'I don't think they actually had newspapers in those times,' Mrs. Ramsbottom commented, as she questioned one child.

'Oh they did,' a girl said. 'Only they were on scrolls and the town crier went round reading out the news to the townsfolk.'

Mrs. Ramsbottom nodded in an impressed sort of way and made notes on her clipboard.

'Marvellous!' Miss Loopney declared to the class. 'Keep up the jolly good work!' She gave them all a big thumbs up, as Mrs. Ramsbottom disappeared out of the door.

With trepidation, Miss Loopney directed the inspector towards upper Key Stage Two. This was where the knights had had the most influence, and she prepared herself to find them up to something outrageous.

But the knights were nowhere to be seen, and all was calm in 5E. 'Where are they?' she hissed to Mr. E.

'I've got them helping with the preparations for the banquet, in the kitchen, out of the way,' he hissed back.

'Good thinking.'

Mrs. Ramsbottom continued into Miss Shurry's class.

'Here we have a medieval kitchen,' Miss Loopney announced.

'And we've been doing a sort of medieval 'Come dine with me' over the last few weeks,' Miss Shurry added.

Mrs. Ramsbottom nodded. 'And what have we out here?' She was looking out onto the kitchen garden and beyond, to where the animals were kept.

'In medieval times people kept animals to slaughter,' a boy announced.

'Indeed they did, young man,' Mrs. Ramsbottom said, looking worriedly at the animals.

'D'you want to come 'n' meet Rollie?' said the boy.

Mrs. Ramsbottom raised her eyebrows. 'Yes' she agreed, with a little twitch of the lips.

Miss Loopney and half the class accompanied them. 'This is Rollie,' said the boy.

'Is he... awaiting slaughter?' Mrs. Ramsbottom enquired.

'No Miss,' the boy piped up. 'He's our pet now. He's really funny.'

As if to prove the boy's point, Rollie wobbled up to the fence and stuck his snout into Mrs. Ramsbottom's hand, taking her by surprise.

'Oh!' she cried and drew back.

Then the pig decided to live up to his name and flopped over, splashing the inspector with mud. He then proceeded to roll back and forth in the mud, much to the children's delight. Miss Loopney gasped, and pulled the inspector back from the fence. She took out her handkerchief and began wiping the mud off the inspector's clothes.

'Don't fuss, Miss Loopney,' said the inspector, swiping the handkerchief away.

Mrs. Ramsbottom smiled at the boy. 'I was brought up on a farm.'

'*Marvellous!*' Miss Loopney cried. 'Shall we return to my office now, to freshen up for lunch?'

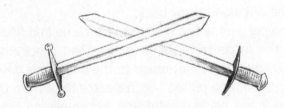

21 The Banquet Begins

Mrs. Diamond knocked on the office door. 'The children are ready for you in the banqueting hall, Miss Loopney.'

'*Marvellous!*' Miss Loopney said. 'We have a sumptuous banquet prepared for you, Mrs. Ramsbottom. You are in for a treat!'

In the dining hall, the tables had been arranged in long rows leading up to the stage, where a special table had been arranged, looking out over the others. The children and teachers sat at the tables waiting quietly.

The inspector looked almost impressed.

'This way ladies,' said Sir Trumpsalot, coming up to them and bowing with a flourish. 'We have a special table for you.'

'This is one of the actors I was telling you about,' Miss Loopney said, introducing Sir Trumpsalot.

'Pleased to meet you,' Mrs. Ramsbottom said, not sounding pleased at all. 'Actually, I would like to sit amongst the children. It will be a good chance for me to speak to them about the school.'

'Of course,' said Miss Loopney. She knew the children loved the school and was not concerned at this.

Sir Trumpsalot looked worried. This was not in the knights' plan to defeat the dragon. How would they slay her, surrounded by children?

Jack and Connor had been listening to this conversation. 'Maybe we could look after the inspector,' Jack said to Miss Loopney.

'Good idea, Jack,' Miss Loopney said, smiling.

'And perchance the lady wouldst like the company of some knights in shining armour,' Sir Trumpsalot said, flashing his most winning smile.

'No, thank you!' the dragon replied, coldly.

'Foiled again!' Sir Trumpsalot muttered, as he retreated to make a new plan with Sir Windibot and Sir Gaseehad.

Jack and Connor escorted the inspector to their table. 'Protect her from the knights, at all costs' Jack whispered to Connor.

Miss Loopney, Mr. E. and several other teachers were seated at the table on the stage.

When Mrs. Ramsbottom was seated, Miss Loopney rose from her seat. 'We welcome Mrs. Ramsbottom today, to our medieval banquet. Let the feasting begin!'

The musicians began to play and various children, who had been chosen as servers, started to dish up bowls of pottage.

In the kitchen the knights were getting in the way of the cooks.

'Do you fine gents have to be here gettin' under our feet?' Mrs. Delaney, the chief cook said.

'We have orders to look after the food for our special guest,' Sir Windibot lied.

'Well, here's her soup. Now get out of our way.' Mrs. Delaney handed Sir Windibot a large bowl of pottage.

'Have you got the special ingredient?' Sir Windibot asked Sir Gaseehad.

Sir Gaseehad slipped his hand into his armour and, checking to see that the cooks were not looking, he dropped a dead mouse into the soup.

'This will be a test to see if she is a real dragon or a real lady. If she is a lady she will shriek and if she is a dragon she will just eat it,' Sir Trumpsalot said.

The knights made a dramatic procession to deliver the soup to the inspector.

'Here they come,' said Connor.

'They're up to something,' Jack whispered. 'Get ready to distract her.'

The knights laid the bowl of pottage in front of the inspector. 'Your starter, My Lady,' Sir Gaseehad said.

'Thank you,' she replied, curtly.

The knights retreated a little way off.

Connor lent over the table to Mrs. Ramsbottom. 'Excuse me, before you eat your soup, can I tell you my nine times table?'

Mrs. Ramsbottom actually beamed. 'Why, of course, young man.'

'One times nine is nine, two nines are eighteen ....

As the inspector took out her clipboard to make notes Jack

quickly swapped her pottage with a girl on the table behind them, who was too busy chatting to notice.

'And twelve nines are one hundred and eight!' said Connor triumphantly.

Aaaagggghhhhh!

A blood-curdling scream came from the girl on the table behind, as she jumped up onto her chair, spilling her pottage, along with the dead mouse, all over her table. Several other girls promptly screamed and jumped on their chairs too.

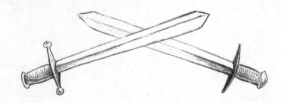

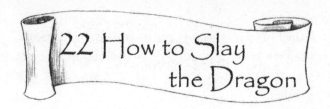

22 How to Slay the Dragon

Miss Loopney stood up to see what the commotion was about. The knights looked confused.

Mr. E. rushed over to take charge of the girls, who were in his class. 'Sit down, girls.' He looked at the dead mouse in horror.

'What is it?' Mrs. Ramsbottom said, turning to look.

'Oh, nothing to worry about,' Mr. E. said, with a fake jolly laugh. 'It's just a bit of odd looking medieval meat. Don't be so silly girls.'

But as he picked up the mouse, by the tail, trying to hide it from the inspector, one of the girls (who was still shrieking and waving her arms about) knocked it out of Mr. E.'s hand. It somersaulted through the air and landed on the inspector's clipboard.

'Sit down girls!' Mr. E. ordered, frantically looking around to see where the mouse had landed.

Jack, seeing where the mouse landed, quickly picked up the clipboard and flipped it; flinging the mouse across the room. The poor creature (you had to feel sorry for it, even though it was dead) came to a final resting place in the white hat on top of the big curly hairdo belonging to Mrs. Delaney, who had popped her head through the serving hatch at a very inopportune moment. She felt a thump on top of her head and put her hand up to investigate. Her hand found the mouse! Mrs. Delaney did not want anyone to see a dead mouse in her kitchen. So, mustering all her self-control, she calmly walked out of the back door, with the creature hidden in her hat, and deposited it in the outside bins.

Mrs. Ramsbottom turned back to her clipboard, which was once again lying innocently on the table. She raised her eyebrows at the children around her, in a way that made some of them giggle.

'They were excellent times tables' she said to Connor, who had totally forgotten about them.

'Would you like to hear a medieval ballad?' Jack asked. 'Our class have been learning one.'

'That would be interesting,' the inspector said.

Jack got up to ask Mr. E. when they could perform it.

Meanwhile the knights were in the kitchen, sulking because the mouse plan hadn't worked.

'Poison!' Sir Windibot said. 'We have to poison the dragon.'

Sir Trumpsalot was beginning to have doubts. 'What if she isn't a dragon in disguise after all?'

'Gadzooks, Trumps!' Sir Gaseehad shouted. 'Of course she is! Everyone is trying to keep her happy so she doesn't destroy Dempsey Road. We need to get rid of her.'

'Well, maybe not something as strong as poison,' Sir Trumpsalot said.

'Be not a wimp!' Sir Gaseehad said, thumping him on the back.

'Prithee, what dost thou mean by a wimp?' Sir Windibot said, turning from the shelves of jars and packets he was looking through.

''Tis a modern word for a coward!' Sir Gaseehad said.

'Darest thou to call me a coward?' Sir Trumpsalot squared himself up for a fight. His hand went to his sword.

'Now, now gents,' Mrs. Delaney said. 'Calm down. There'll be none of that in my kitchen. If you're going to be in here, make yourselves useful, and pour more drinks for the special guest. And help to serve the food. This roast gammon needs plating up!'

The knights backed down. They had never been bossed around by a woman, and were shocked. Sir Trumpsalot began putting gammon on plates, Sir Gaseehad found a bottle of red wine. Sir Windibot went back to looking through the shelves, when suddenly he cried, 'Zounds! I've got it!'

He sidled over to the other two, so that Mrs. Delaney wouldn't be suspicious. In his hand he held a jar. On it were the words 'So hot it will blow your head off!'

'And look here, he said, pointing further down the jar. 'Chilli powder to make you breathe fire.'

'Wow!' Sir Gaseehad said, breaking into 21st-century speak.

'Go for it, dudes! Let's put this magical powder in her wine and see if she breathes fire.'

'Dost thou really want a fire breathing dragon to reveal herself in the banqueting hall?' Sir Trumpsalot said.

'But it saith it shall blow off her head!' Sir Windibot persisted. 'We should try it.'

Sir Trumpsalot had visions of the woman's head exploding and spraying pieces of hair, teeth, brain and spectacles all over the hall.

'I agree with Windi,' Sir Gaseehad said.

'Be it on your heads,' Sir Trumpsalot said.

'Nay sir, it will be off with her head when this potion does its work!' Sir Windibot cried.

Sir Gaseehad guffawed with laughter.

'Hey, you lot! Get a move on with those meals!' Mrs. Delaney shouted.

Sir Windibot poured a large amount of the chilli powder into a goblet of red wine and swilled it around. Sir Trumpsalot picked up a plate of food and the knights then made their way, in grand procession, out of the kitchen.

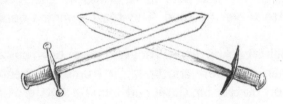

23 A Fire Breathing Dragon

Mr. E. had told Jack that they could sing the medieval ballad as the inspector was eating her meal. So all of 5E were now assembled at the front of the dining hall.

'Oh no! What are they up to now?' Jack groaned. Sir Gaseehad was carrying the goblet high in the air, as if it were the crown jewels.

'There's something nasty in that goblet,' Jack whispered to Connor. 'We've got to get over there!'

'And now,' Mr. E. announced, 'for your delight and entertainment, 5E will sing Greensleeves.' He took a flourishing bow before turning to the class. 'One, two, three, one, two, three ...'

Jack and Connor's eyes were fixed on the knights, as Sir Gaseehad bent to present the goblet to Mrs. Ramsbottom. 'Come on Connor, we have to go - now!'

But as they were about to step out of the ranks, to Jack's relief, he saw the inspector shaking her head and refusing the goblet.

'Phew! She doesn't want it,' Connor said in between singing.

But Sir Gaseehad was not one to give up. Jack cringed as the knight went down on bended knee and took Mrs. Ramsbottom's hand, about to kiss it.

'Urgh! Wish he wouldn't do that!' Jack said.

Miss Loopney, who had been lost in a moment's relief, on hearing the sweet singing of 5E, suddenly noticed Sir Gaseehad too. She was not pleased at his advances towards Mrs. Ramsbottom, and began making her way down from the stage.

The next few moments were like another action-scene-in-slow-motion, from a movie.

5E ploughed on with the song. Sir Gaseehad kissed the inspector's hand. Miss Loopney saw this and marched towards him. Connor and Jack held their breath. Mrs. Ramsbottom blushed almost purple and grinned hideously at Sir Gaseehad. She lifted the goblet to her lips.

Jack couldn't help himself. **'Noooooooooooo!'**

He launched himself towards the inspector's table as Mrs. Ramsbottom took a big gulp of the wine.

At that moment Miss Loopney reached the inspector. 'Sir Gaseehad, I really don't think it is appropriate ....'

She didn't get to finish because Mrs. Ramsbottom spewed the whole contents of the goblet all over her like a power-washer.

'FIRE!' she screeched. **'I'm on FIRE!'**

The knights jumped up and down.

HUZZAH! HUZZAH!

Their victorious shouting was accompanied by the sounds of loud parping. But they were oblivious to it, in their triumph!

'When is the dragon's head going to explode?' Sir Windibot shouted.

'Just wait for it,' Sir Gaseehad laughed.

Miss Loopney just stood there, in shock, dripping red wine like blood.

5E had stopped singing, and were gawping at the scene.

Mr. E. rushed over. The inspector was gasping for breath and turning an extreme shade of purple.

'Get her some water!' Mr. E. yelled.

Jack picked up a jug from the nearest table. He raced over and without thinking, poured it all over her. This made her gasp and splutter even more.

'Don't put her out, thou looby!' cried Sir Windibot. 'She is about to explode!'

'She needs to drink it, Jack. Not wear it!' Mr. E. shouted.

Another teacher brought more water and the inspector began to gulp it down. She drank enough to fill a reservoir.

Miss Loopney had not moved. She was rooted to the spot as if someone had turned her into a statue.

Mr E. turned to the knights. 'What are you trying to do?'

Innocently, Sir Windibot replied, 'Why, slay the dragon, of course.'

'Don't you get it?' Mr. E. stormed.

'Cool it dude!' Sir Gaseehad said, as Mr. E. looked more and more like he was the one about to explode.

'I will *not* cool it, Sir Gaseehad! Get out of here, all of you! We thought you could save this school, but all you have done is guarantee it's ruin!'

The room had gone silent, apart from the coughing and gasping of the inspector. The knights were speechless. With heads hung in shame, they clanked out of the dining hall, trumping uncontrollably as they left.

The inspector was still downing water, as if she had found the only oasis in a desert. Miss Loopney uttered a pitiful whimper and fell to the floor, with no knight in shining armour to catch her.

'*We're doomed!*' were her last words.

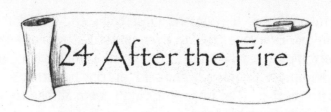

24 After the Fire

The knights spent the next week holed up in their shed. They wouldn't come out, even when Jack's mum tried to coax them with their favourite 21st century delicacy; double cheese burger and chips. She just left trays of food by the door for them. Loud parping noises came from the shed constantly, as the knights had given in to the curse and no longer bothered to keep it under control.

Jack tried to speak to them through the door every day, but they wouldn't let him in.

'Go away, Jack!' Sir Windibot said, for the fifth time that evening. 'We don't want to see anyone.'

Connor was with him. 'Come on Sir Windi, you have to come out at some point. You can't stay in there forever. And the smell must be... Well...'

'Go away!' the three knights chorused.

Connor, Jack, his mum and dad sat round the Wobbly Table in the kitchen. 'What are we going to do?' Jack said.

'Do you mean about the knights or the school?' Dad asked.

'Both.'

*

In the aftermath of the dragon's visit, a rain cloud of utter misery hung over the school. Miss Loopney wandered round in a daze, trying to keep alive her everything-will-be-fine smile, but the children could tell by the way she said *marvellous* in such a tiny, dismal voice, that all was not well.

Mr. E. was not his usual bouncy self. All the medieval displays were taken down, leaving the classrooms and corridors bare and lifeless. Everyone tried to liven up Mr. E., but not even the class attempt at a joke contest produced a smile from him.

'Cheer up, Mr. E.,' Maisey had said, putting her arm round her favourite teacher. 'The inspector didn't seem all bad to me.'

Mr. E. just shook his head.

When Jack and Connor went to school on Friday, one week after the dragon's visit, Miss Loopney came into their classroom with an envelope in her hand. Her face was pale. 'Can I have a word, Mr. E.?'

She took Mr. E. into a corner and showed him the envelope. 'I daren't open it. It's from the inspector. This is the moment when we lose our jobs. How am I going to break it to the staff?'

At that moment Mrs. Diamond came rushing into the room. 'I've got the press on the phone, Miss Loopney. I think they've got wind of the inspection outcome. They want to talk to you.'

'Oh dear!' Miss Loopney sighed, and followed Mrs. Diamond back up the corridor.

'Are you really going to lose your job Mr. E.?' Jack asked.

'You shouldn't have been listening Jack, but yes, probably.'

'No way!' said Connor, 'You are an ace teacher!'

'We're sorry about the knights,' Jack said. 'I should never have brought them to school.'

'You weren't to know what would happen. And I don't think the knights really meant any harm. They genuinely thought Mrs. Ramsbottom was the enemy.'

'Well she is, isn't she, Mr. E.?' Connor said.

'Sort of,' Mr. E. replied.

'The knights are really sorry. They won't come out of the shed ...I mean their room.'

Mr. E. sighed. 'What a mess. And the crazy thing is, all any of us wants is the best for Dempsey Road Primary.'

'Even the knights,' Jack said.

Mr. E. smiled at him. 'Yep, I know.'

'Is this some kind of cruel joke?' Miss Loopney said, down the phone to the reporter.

'Not at all!' he replied. 'We want to make Dempsey Road an example to the whole town.'

'A laughing stock, you mean!' Miss Loopney stormed. 'Now I'll thank you to go away!' She slammed the phone down on her desk. Mrs. Diamond jumped.

The phone began ringing again. 'Grrrrr! Get rid of him for me, will you?'

'Delighted to!' said the secretary, picking up the phone, and heading to her own office.

Miss Loopney sat with her elbows on the desk, head in hands. All the years she had given to Dempsey Road. Years of hard work, long hours, problem solving and most of all - love. For it all to come to this was just too much.

'Erm... Miss Loopney, That Mrs. Ramsbottom is on the phone,' Mrs. Diamond said, popping her head back around the door.

The head teacher looked up. 'I'd better take it.'

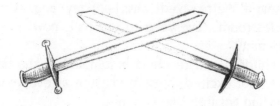

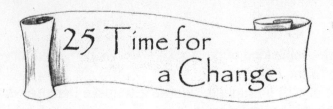

25 Time for a Change

'Yes, I will, Mrs. Ramsbottom. Goodbye.'

Miss Loopney put down the phone, and slowly picked up the envelope again. She looked at it as if it would bite her, then ripped it open, ferociously.

She read the letter over and over again.

Then, she jumped from her seat and whooped the loudest whoop you've ever heard coming from a head teacher's office.

WHOOOOOOOOPPEEEEEEEEEE!

Leaping out into the corridor, she ran into Mrs. Diamond's office, clasping the astonished secretary in a breath-stealing bear-hug.

'We're saved!' she cried. 'Read this!' She thrust the letter at Mrs. Diamond. 'Call that reporter back. Get him here! Oh, and call Jack's mum. Get those knights here too - immediately!'

'We're saved! We're saved!' Miss Loopney sang, as she danced to every classroom. 'Everyone to the hall, now! I'm calling a special assembly.'

All the children and teachers assembled in the hall. There was a quiet, but excited, buzz of chatter, as everyone tried to guess what had got into Miss Loopney.

'She really has gone loopy now,' Mr. E. said to Miss Shurry.

'What do you think's happened?' Connor said to Jack.

'I dunno. One minute she looks like the world is about to be hit by an asteroid, and the next she sounds like she's won the lottery!'

Miss Loopney had gone back to her office to compose herself, in order to address the children. As she entered the hall though,

she couldn't contain her excitement.

'My lovely children and teachers. It's absolutely, fantastically, wonderfully *marvellous*! We are not doomed at all. The school has received an 'outstanding' grade from the inspector! Mrs. Ramsbottom loved us.'

The teachers looked at each other in disbelief.

'Let me read you the letter:

Dear Miss Loopney,

After an eventful day at Dempsey Road Primary School last Friday, I have come to the conclusion that you are an outstanding school. Your sense of adventure and enthusiasm shone through. The children were completely engaged in all the activities. They were learning so much about medieval times. And in such innovative and ingenious ways. I thought you were very brave to stage a jousting tournament and to include me in the drama, as if I were an enemy, attacking the castle. The moat was a very courageous idea. To quote your lovely phrase – Marvellous!

I don't know what came over me at lunch time. I apologise for my coughing outburst, and hope your suit recovers. Perhaps the medieval herbs and spices didn't agree with me. Let's keep it between ourselves that I was drinking wine!

'Oh dear!' said Miss Loopney, 'I didn't mean to read that bit out. Back to the letter:'

One of the things that most impressed me, was the kindness shown to me by that young girl who helped me up and brought me a glass of water, after my little mishap at the jousting tournament.

I would like to recommend that your school become a centre for excellence in using drama in the curriculum. I thought your theatre troupe were incredibly convincing as knights and obviously brought another dimension to the proceedings.

I hope you will invite me back when you do another dramatic day.

Yours sincerely,

Mrs. Ramsbottom
Schools' Inspector

'*Marvellous* isn't it, my dears?'

At that moment, Sir Trumpsalot, Sir Windibot and Sir Gaseehad clanked into the assembly, heads bent, carrying their helmets under their arms. They knelt before Miss Loopney.

'Dear Lady Loopney,' Sir Trumpsalot began, 'Verily, we are most sorry for our misdemeanours. We are your humble servants ....'

'Get up, get up,' Miss Loopney said. 'You have saved our school after all!' And she gave them all a big sloppy kiss on the cheeks.

The whole room erupted into clapping, cheering and whooping.

The knights stood up, and looked around at the smiling, laughing faces. Sir Windibot let out a massive you-know-what in his excitement.

PTTTHHHHHHTTTTTT!

'Beg pardon, Miss Loopney,' he said.

'Oh don't worry, Sir Windi. No one cares about your little problem today. You are heroes!' She let out a longer than usual burst of Star Wars laughter.

Ha-Ha Ha- Haaaaaaaaaa Ha!
Ha-Ha Ha-Haaaaaaaaaaa Ha!

'Saints alive! We did it!' Sir Trumpsalot said. 'We defeated the dragon.'

'You tamed the dragon, Sir Trumpsalot,' said Miss Loopney. She held the knights' hands in the air like heroes, and the cheering went on and on and on and on and on.

The press came and took photographs of the knights, teachers and all the children. The story was reported in the local papers and Miss Loopney had lots of phone calls from new parents wanting to get their children into Dempsey Road Primary School.

*

It was decided that the school needed a little break from the knights. Miss Loopney promised to invite them back when the school was ready to do its next big production.

'What shall we do now?' Sir Trumpsalot said on Saturday, as he and the other knights sat around the Wobbly Table with Jack and Connor. 'We have fulfilled our mission at Dempsey Road but we are still stuck here in the 21st century.'

'We must try to find a way back to our own time, and rid ourselves of this curse,' Sir Windibot said.

'I wish you didn't have to leave,' Jack said.

'We may be around for some time, Jack, as I know not how we can get back to medieval times,' Sir Trumpsalot said.

'You're local heroes, so maybe you should make the most of that for a while,' Connor said.

'We accept the honour with humble thanks!' Sir Gaseehad said. He stood up and drew his sword. Sir Windibot and Sir Trumpsalot joined him, making a pyramid with their swords. And together they chorused:

'To the Knights of the Wobbly Table!'

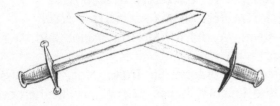

Paaarp!

Glossary of Knightly Words and Phrases

Abode: Place to live

Adieu: Goodbye

Alas: Oh dear, we're in trouble now!

Anon: See you soon

Art: Are

Break your fast: We get the word breakfast from this phrase. A fast was where you didn't eat for a long time, like overnight. When you ate in the morning you broke your fast – breakfast.

By my faith! Trust me!

Chivalrous/Chivalry: Knights' code of honour

Crusades: Missions that knights would go on. Involved lots of fighting.

Damsel: A young girlie, a damsel in distress!

Dost: Do (eg: dost thou know = do you know)

Doublet: Medieval jacket worn by noblemen

Dulcimer: Horizontal instrument with strings, ancestor of a piano

Fare thee well: Goodbye

Fie upon you!: A medieval insult (interpret as you will)

Forsooth: In truth, in fact, indeed

Gadzooks!: Flippin' 'eck!

Garderobe: A medieval toilet (as Mum explained!)

Gauntlet: A narrow passageway

God's breath: Blimey!

Grave: Serious

Hose: Medieval tights worn by a nobleman

Hovel: A very poor place to live

Huzzah!: Hurray!

In truth: In fact

Jousting: A medieval tournament. Knights on horseback carrying lances tried to knock each other off as they galloped towards each other at break-neck speed.

Knave: Boy (usually cheeky or naughty)

Looby: Fool

Lute: Stringed instrument, ancestor of the guitar

Mead: A common drink, made of honey water, grain and spices. A little alcoholic!

Methinks: I think

Per chance: Perhaps

Pray tell me: Please tell me

Prithee: Please

Psalteries: Stringed instruments, like a small harps

Saith: Says, said

Saints alive!: Oh my goodness!

Solar: A private room in a castle

Steed: Horse

Tabor: Drum

Thou: You (subject of sentence)

Thee: You (object of sentence)

Thy: Your

Verily: Absolutely, truly

What ho!: Hey there!

Wherefore: Why

Zounds!: Wow!

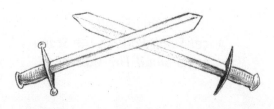

About Karen ...

Karen lives near York with her husband and two children. One of her favourite things to do as a child, was to draw lots of stick families and make up stories about them. It's a good job she is a writer now, not an illustrator!

Being a teacher provided Karen with lots of inspiration for several of her books; especially this one. As she was editing this book she enjoyed trying out funny voices for the characters. She is looking forward to writing the next adventure for the knights.

Karen loves to hear from readers and always replies to emails. Please contact her on her website: *www.karenlangtree.com*

Other books by Karen:
(Published by OneWay Press)

My Wicked Stepmother
Fairy Rescuers
Return to Elysia
Breaking Silence

Other publications by Karen and Gill:
(Published by Monkey Island Publishing)

Angel Small
Angel Small Follows the Star
Angel Small The Musical

About Gill ...

Gill has illustrated and designed many children's books, and is delighted to have teamed up with Karen to bring a whole new perspective to her portfolio.

Gill was brought up in rural Lancashire and spent most of her childhood drawing and exploring the hills and streams in wellies. To this day she maintains an interest in all things wiggly. Her most beloved places are hilly and woody, so living in the Yorkshire Dales is most enjoyable, especially with her husband and two children.

Together Gill and Karen
have created Monkey Island Publishing
to bring you stories in word, pictures and song.
For more information, go to:

www.monkeyislandpublishing.com

'Children will love this fun romp where old meets new.'

Andy Seed, winner of the Blue Peter Book Award 2015, author of Prankenstein, The Silly Book of Side-splitting Stuff, and more...

'We just finished reading *Knights of the Wobbly Table* as a bedtime story. We loved it. Kept us on the edge of our seats!'

Sam Hargreaves, Ella's dad

'The opening lines were so good I wanted to read the whole book to my grandson.'

Marshall Rankin, Hamish's grandad

'I thought the knights were really funny. I wish we had some at my school. I want to know what they are going to get up to next.'

Joseph Aged 8

112